Mary C Innes

A Memoir of William Wolseley

Admiral of the Red Squadron

Mary C Innes

A Memoir of William Wolseley
Admiral of the Red Squadron

ISBN/EAN: 9783337319151

Printed in Europe, USA, Canada, Australia, Japan

Cover: Foto ©Raphael Reischuk / pixelio.de

More available books at **www.hansebooks.com**

A MEMOIR OF
ADMIRAL WOLSELEY

CHAPTER I

Admiral William Wolseley, the subject of the present memoir, was descended from one of the most ancient of the Staffordshire families. His ancestors are said to have been seated in that county before the Conquest; and it has been stated by a learned genealogist of the present day, that "the Wolseleys of Wolseley have held their lands unbrokenly since Alfred the Great first wore the crown of united England."

The surname is evidently of Saxon origin; and according to an old family tradition—borne out by their Armorial Bearings [1]—"Wolf-slayer" was the *sobriquet* given by his friends and neighbours to an ancestor of the family renowned for his prowess in slaying the wolves, with which the country was in those days infested. The lands of this mighty hunter became known by the name of "Wolveslea"; [2]

[1] The Arms of the family of Wolseley are—*arg.*, a talbot, passant gu. The Crest is—Out of a ducal coronet, *or*, a wolf's head ppr.

[2] Or, "the field of wolves."

A

and some centuries later, when surnames were generally adopted, his descendants, as was the case with many other ancient Houses, took theirs from the lands in their possession.

In 1066, the year in which William, Duke of Normandy, conquered England, the family estate was held by "Siward, lord of Wolseley"; whose descendant,

Robert Wolseley, living in the reign of Charles I., was created a Baronet in 1628. Sir Robert married Mary Wroughton, daughter of Sir George Wroughton of Wilcot, County Wilts. And Admiral Wolseley, in consequence of being descended from that family, was entitled to trace—in a well-authenticated line—descent from Lionel Plantagenet, Duke of Clarence, third son of King Edward III.[1] Sir Robert's son,

Sir Charles Wolseley, the second Baronet, was M.P. for Staffordshire in the reigns of Charles I. and II. He was on the side of the Parliament, however, during the Civil Wars, and was one of Oliver Cromwell's Privy Council of Sixteen, and is said to have been a man of very superior talent. He wrote a book on the "Unreasonableness of Atheism," which gained him very great credit with "The Protector," who, it is reported, suggested the subject for him to write upon. Sir Charles married

---

[1] Admiral Wolseley's descent from Edward III. is entered in Foster's "Royal Lineage of our Noble and Gentle Families." (See Descent of Sir Clement Wolseley, Bart.)

Anne Fiennes,[1] daughter of Lord Saye and Sele ; and their youngest son,

Captain Richard Wolseley, the Admiral's great-grandfather, was in the service of William III. in Ireland, where he acquired by purchase a portion of the estate of Charles Butler, Earl of Arran. He settled at Mount Arran, now Mount Wolseley, County Carlow, and was M.P. for the Borough of Carlow. Captain Wolseley married Frances, daughter and heiress of John Burneston, Esq., and had three surviving sons. The eldest,[1]

William Wolseley, became the fifth Baronet of the English branch, and succeeded to the family estate in Staffordshire on the death of his uncle, Sir Henry Wolseley. Sir William was ancestor of the successive baronets of that line, and is now represented by the present proprietor of Wolseley Hall, Sir Charles Michael Wolseley, ninth Baronet. Captain Richard Wolseley's second son,

Robert Wolseley, the Admiral's grandfather, married a Miss Waring, daughter of a gentleman settled in the County Kilkenny. According to Sir Bernard Burke, Mrs. Wolseley's mother, Mrs. Waring, was a lady of the family of Neville; and through her, he said, Admiral Wolseley was again entitled to claim royal descent. Mr. and Mrs. Robert Wolseley had a son, William Neville

[1] As this lady was descended from Agnes, sister of William of Wykeham, Bishop of Winchester, the Wolseleys and their descendants are entitled to claim, as " Founder's kin," free education at Winchester College, and at New College, Oxford.

Wolseley, who was the Admiral's father. Captain
Richard Wolseley's third son,

Richard Wolseley, the Admiral's grand-uncle, was
left the estate of Mount Wolseley by his father. He
was M.P. for Carlow, and was created a Baronet in
1744. He was ancestor of the distinguished soldier,
Field-Marshal the Viscount Wolseley, and of all the
baronets of the Irish branch, and is now represented
by the present Sir Capel Charles Wolseley.

About the year 1750, Admiral Wolseley's father,
William Neville Wolseley, who was then a captain
in the 47th, was serving with his regiment in
Nova Scotia; and he there made the acquaintance
of Miss Anne Cosby, the lady to whom he was
shortly afterwards married. Besides the subject of
the present memoir, who was Captain and Mrs.
Wolseley's second son, they had another son, Mr.
Robert Wolseley, who married his second cousin,
Miss Anne Winniett, granddaughter of Judge
Winniett. Captain and Mrs Wolseley had also
two daughters—Elizabeth, married to —— Lam-
phier, Esq., R.N., and Anne, who died at an early
age unmarried.

The ancient family of Cosby, from which Admiral
Wolseley was descended on his mother's side, was
said by Sir Bernard Burke to have been also of
Saxon origin, and is stated to have possessed the
lordship of Cosby, County Leicester, previously to
the Norman Conquest.

Francis Cosbie, the first member of his House

who settled in Ireland, came over in the time of Queen Mary. He was an active defender of the Pale, and was appointed by patent in 1558 General of the Kerne, and in 1562 was granted the site of the suppressed Abbey of Stradbally. His eldest son,

Alexander Cosbie of Stradbally Abbey, who also obtained very extensive grants of lands in the Queen's County, married Dorcas, daughter of William Sydney of Otford, County Kent, Maid of Honour to Queen Elizabeth. Mr. Cosbie's second son, Richard, eventually succeeded to the family property, and was direct ancestor of Mrs. Wolseley's grandfather, Alexander Cosby, of Stradbally Hall, whose eldest son,

Dudley Cosby, succeeded to the property on the death of his father in 1694, and was M.P. for Queen's County, and also Lieutenant-Colonel of the county militia. His son, Mr. Pole Cosby—first-cousin of Mrs. Wolseley—succeeded him, and was father of—

Dudley Alexander Sydney Cosby of Stradbally Hall, second cousin of Admiral Wolseley. Mr. Cosby was minister plenipotentiary to the court of Denmark, and was in 1768 created a Peer of Ireland as Baron Sydney of Leix. In December 1773 Lord Sydney married Lady Isabella St. Lawrence, daughter of the first Earl of Howth; but as he died in the ensuing month, 17th January 1774, his peerage became extinct, and the property was then inherited by his cousin, Admiral Phillips Cosby, Mrs. Wolseley's brother.

Mrs. Wolseley had many relations in America; and some of them were, in the early part of the eighteenth century, holding important government appointments there. One of her uncles, Lieutenant-General William Cosby, was Governor of New York and the Jerseys. He was also Colonel of the Royal Irish Regiment, and was equerry to the Queen. He married Lady Grace Montagu, sister of the Earl of Halifax, and left at his decease, in 1736, two sons and two daughters.[1]

An aunt of Mrs. Wolseley—the General's sister —Elizabeth Cosby, was married to Lieutenant-General Richard Philipps, Governor of Nova Scotia. This lady died before her husband, leaving a son, who was ancestor of the present Sir James Philipps, Bart., of Picton Castle, County Pembroke. General Philipps died in 1750, aged ninety, and was buried in Westminster Abbey. His brother-in-law,

Lieutenant - Colonel Alexander Cosby — Mrs. Wolseley's father—was the fifth son of Mr. A. Cosby of Stradbally Hall. He held the appointment of Lieutenant-Governor of Nova Scotia till his death, on the 26th December 1743. His wife, Anne Winniett—Admiral Wolseley's maternal grandmother, — was a daughter of Alexander Winniett, Esq., of Annapolis Royal.[2] Besides

---

[1] General Cosby's eldest daughter—Mrs. Wolseley's cousin-german —Elizabeth, married Lord Augustus Fitzroy, and was mother of the third Duke of Grafton, and of Lieutenant-General Charles Fitzroy, created Baron Southampton in 1780.

[2] Mrs. Cosby was a sister of Judge Winniett, of Annapolis Royal.

their daughter Mrs. Wolseley, Colonel and Mrs. Cosby had two others—Elizabeth, wife of Captain Foye, and Mary, who married, first, Captain Charles Cotterill, and, secondly, Captain John Buchanan, R.N. They had also two sons; the eldest, William, a captain in the army, was killed and scalped by the Indians in 1748. Their second son,

Philipps Cosby, who will be frequently mentioned in these pages, was in the navy. In 1774, *Captain* Cosby—as he had then been for some years—succeeded to the family property, Stradbally Hall, on the death of his cousin, Lord Sydney. But apparently being too fond of his profession to exchange an active naval life for the somewhat less exciting one of a country gentleman, he continued to serve for many years afterwards, and commanded the *Centaur*, of seventy-four guns, on the 27th July 1778, in an engagement with the French, in which his nephew, William Wolseley, took part as junior lieutenant of the *Duke*, ninety-eight guns.

In another engagement fought on the 16th March 1781, between the British squadron under Admiral Arbuthnot and the French fleet off the coast of America, Captain Cosby led the van, in the *Robust*, of seventy-four guns, the ship he then commanded. And, according to the naval historian, Dr. Campbell, that vessel "bore the brunt of

One of Mrs. Cosby's sisters married General Amherst. Her other sisters were Mrs. Handfield and Mrs. Howe. A daughter of the Judge —a first cousin of Mrs. Wolseley—married Lieutenant James Nunn, of the 57th Regiment, in which he served all through the American war.

the engagement ; " and the Doctor further adds
that "the *Robust* had far more than her proportion of killed and wounded, and by having at one
time three ships upon her, her masts, rigging, sails,
and boats were torn to pieces."

Captain Cosby was promoted to the rank of Vice-
Admiral, at some period between the years 1785
and 1789, when he had command of the fleet
in the Mediterranean ; and his nephew, William
Wolseley, during those years, was captain of his
uncle's flagship, the *Trusty*.

On the 19th September 1790, on Admiral Cosby's
appointment as Commander-in-Chief on the Irish
coast, it was unanimously voted by "the Mayor,
Sheriffs, and Common Council of the City of Corke,"
that "the freedom at large thereof" was to be presented to him "in a silver box, as public testimony of the very high opinion they entertain of his
merit, and the great satisfaction they feel in the
appointment of so gallant and deserving an officer
to that station."

Of Admiral Cosby's further services it is not
necessary to say more at present, as they will be
mentioned in connection with those of his nephew.
Having held several other important appointments,
he retired from the navy, with the rank of Admiral
of the White—I think, about the year 1794—and
settled at his family seat, Stradbally Hall.

He represented the Queen's County in the Irish
Parliament, known as "Grattan's Parliament," and

was apparently an M.P. in 1790, as his portrait appears in a picture, painted by H. Barrand and J. Hayter, of "The Irish House of Commons, A.D. 1790."

In 1792 Admiral Cosby married Elizabeth, daughter of William Gunthorpe, Esq. ; but having died childless in the beginning of 1808, he was succeeded by a distant relation, Mr. Thomas Cosby of Vicarstown, ancestor of Colonel Cosby, J.P. and D.L., the present proprietor of Stradbally Hall.

Having completed these preliminary notes, which I am afraid may be considered rather tedious by the general reader, it only remains to be said, before beginning my account of Admiral Wolseley's life, that these details concerning his ancestry and re- lations have been given, as they may interest his descendants, and others more distantly connected with his family, who may perhaps have been previously unacquainted with some of the facts mentioned here.

Admiral Wolseley was born on the 15th of March 1756, at Annapolis Royal, Nova Scotia. In a memorandum written for his youngest son, Mr. Cosby Wolseley, he says :—" In the year 1746 the French and Indians, being in possession of Nova Scotia *in part*, were at war with us ; we had Halifax, Annapolis, and some other places, but held by force of our troops. I *believe* Lord Amherst commanded. My father, whose name was William Neville

Wolseley, was either a captain or lieutenant in the
47th Regiment, at or near that time at Annapolis,
where they had a fort."

The country was almost entirely wood, from
whence they were, Admiral Wolseley adds, "con-
tinually annoyed by the French and Indians."
"There was," he says, "continued intercourse with
New York, where the Governor was Alexander
Cosby, with a large family. My mother was his
second daughter, and married my father some time
about the year 1751, and lived at the fort of Annapolis Royal. I think (for I have no document) that
my brother Robert must have been born at Annapolis Royal about the year 1753, and I was born
on the 15th March 1756, at Annapolis Royal ; my
sisters were also born there.

"The garrison was strong in troops ; and Colonel
Handfield's family, Major Williams, and Alexander
Howe were all our relations. After the death of
Governor Cosby, his widow came and settled at
Annapolis among her daughters—my mother, Mrs.
Foy, and Mrs. Cotterill. My uncle, Philipps Cosby,
went into the navy. As the success of our troops
gave confidence, the superior officers built the town
of Annapolis, and Mrs. Cosby became possessed of
many houses and much cleared land there."

In the year 1759 Nova Scotia was the scene of
very stirring events, as the great naval and military
operations were in progress which ended in 1760 in
the conquest of Canada. In the year 1759 Admiral

Wolseley says :—"General Wolfe and Admiral Sir Charles Saunders, with a body of troops, came out and took Louisbourg and Cape Bréton. My father's regiment, the 47th, or part of it, was ordered to Halifax, where our family removed to. My father was at an outside fort, called the Eastern Battery, right opposite to the town of Halifax, at the other side of the harbour. He got a grant of land there, and built some out-offices. And I remember living in the battery! This property was lost by my father (for debt), and he was obliged to sell out, and came home in the *Wasp* sloop-of-war, leaving my mother and four children to follow." And he adds :—"It was in the year 1764 that we came home from America. My mother went to Halifax to get her passage home ; not finding a ship, she was advised to go to St. John's, Newfoundland, where Captain Charles Saxton, of the navy, was kind enough to allow her and her children a passage home in his ship, the *Pearl* frigate, and we arrived safe at Portsmouth, from whence we went through Bath to Bristol, to join my father in Ireland.[1]

"A short time afterwards," he continues, "I was put to school at the College of Kilkenny, under Doctor Hewson. I think I was there about two years ;" and he adds, "My grandmother and aunt lived at Kilkenny. After this I was put on

[1] These and other details are taken partly from the memorandum already referred to, and partly from a short memoir, written from Admiral Wolseley's dictation by his daughter, Mrs. Innes.

board the *Goodwill* cutter, in the year 1769, at
Passage, Waterford ; Lieutenant John Buchanan
commanding the cutter.   Lieutenant John Buchanan
married my aunt." And he says, in the memorandum :—" My brother, Robert Wolseley, first went
to sea with my uncle, but, disliking the navy, came
home ; and I was taken from school and went with
him.   I did duty as midshipman rather more than
two years on board the *Goodwill*."

"Sometime during that period I went in the
cutter's boat as an observer of the impressing of
seamen, on account of the Falkland Islands disturb-
ances." (England was preparing to go to war with
Spain about these islands.) "We boarded a billingder full of people, who had been employed in
the Newfoundland fisheries, and who were determined not to be pressed, and had previously risen
and confined the master and his mate. They beat
the men of the *Goodwill* cutter's boat, and threw
them, and me along with them, all overboard ; and
then ran the billingder on shore, right under Bally-
hack church, and from her got ashore, and all
escaped into the county of Wexford. No lives
were lost. I and some of the men swam very well.
The *Goodwill* was paid off at Sheerness, and I then
went to my uncle in London, Captain Philipps
Cosby, of the navy,[1] who placed me at Mr. Wad-
dington's, in Downing Street, Westminster, who
kept a naval school." (Here, according to the

---

[1] Afterwards Admiral of the White.

memorandum, Admiral Wolseley remained for a year; but, according to the memoir, only for seven or eight months.)

The *Portland*, 50-gun ship, was then going to be fitted out for the purpose of changing ships at Jamaica, with the Commodore, Sir George Rodney —afterwards Lord Rodney—whose ship, the *Princess Amelia*, of eighty guns, was an old vessel which had a narrow escape of foundering on the voyage home. Admiral Wolseley says:—"The *Portland* on going out was commanded by Captain John Barclay, and was principally manned by guardships. One of the lieutenants was Waldegrave, afterwards Lord Radstock; George Bowen, late admiral, was another. I went out in the *Portland* as a midshipman, and was placed under the famous Collingwood —afterwards Lord Collingwood — who was then mate; and Lord Hugh Seymour Conway and Lord Hervey were in the same mess.

"We changed ships at Jamaica, and sailed from thence for England in the *Princess Amelia* round Cuba and through the Straits of Bahama; and we met a heavy gale of wind on entering the banks of Newfoundland. The ship was very nearly lost on this occasion, by broaching-to; and the courses blowing out of the bolt-ropes and springing a leak in the forefoot, all hands were put to the pumps. This accident of broaching-to was caused by a blunderbuss falling out of the gun-room, jamming the tiller and preventing the ship's steering. Most fortunately the next day was calm, and by very great exertions the guns were got aft, and the ship lightened forward as much as it was possible; by which means they got at the leak, and found a plank started at the butt end. This was then secured by being soldered and covered with lead, so that no further accident happened, and we arrived safe at Portsmouth, when the ship was paid off."

In 1773 Mr. Wolseley went as midshipman on board the *Salisbury*, fifty guns, under Commodore Sir Edward Hughes, and sailed for the East Indies. The *Seahorse*, 20-gun ship (on board of which were Lord Nelson and Sir Thomas Troubridge as young midshipmen), sailed with them. They touched at Madeira and the Cape of Good Hope, arrived at Madras, and found Sir Robert Harland, whom they were to relieve. Mr. Wolseley was five years out in this vessel (the *Salisbury*), and on his return to England, the first American war and the French war having just commenced, he was appointed a lieutenant, in the fleet commanded by Lord Keppel and Sir Hugh Palliser.

He says in the memoir written by Mrs. Innes, from his own dictation :—" There being great want of young officers for a squadron of ten sail of the line immediately wanted by Admiral Keppel (afterwards Lord Keppel) to meet the French on equal terms in the Channel, where they had come up and driven him in, I was one of the sixteen who were ordered up to London from the *Salisbury* to pass our examination ; we were made lieutenants, and immediately sent down to the line of battle-ships fitting out. I was appointed youngest lieu-tenant to the *Duke*, ninety-eight guns, and joined her at Plymouth, and two days afterwards sailed with Keppel's fleet of twenty-seven sail of the line, and was in action in the following month with the French fleet of thirty-two sail of the line, in the battle that took place on the 27th July 1778."

The following account of the engagement is taken from Dr. Campbell's "Naval History of Great Britain":—"The French fleet," he says, "consisting of thirty-two ships of the line and a number of frigates, was divided into three squad-rons, under Count D'Orvilliers, commander-in-chief, and the Duke De Chartres, a prince of the blood, assisted by three other admirals.

"The British fleet was also divided into three squadrons, commanded by Admiral Keppel ; the vice-admirals, Sir Robert Harland and Sir Hugh Palliser. The two fleets came within sight of each other in the afternoon of the 23rd of July, in the Bay of Biscay, about thirty-five leagues to the west-ward of Brest.

"On the 24th the British admiral threw out the signal to chase to windward, which was con-tinued the two following days, in order to seize the first opportunity of bringing the enemy to a close engagement ; but this proved ineffectual, the

French cautiously avoiding coming to an action, and in their manœuvres showing great address and nautical knowledge.

"About four o'clock in the morning of the 27th July, the French were discovered to windward, about five miles distance. Admiral Keppel, finding some of his fleet too much scattered, made signals to collect them together, still continuing to follow the enemy. About ten o'clock a heavy dark squall came on, which continued nearly an hour; when it cleared up, the two fleets, by a shift of wind, had neared each other, but on different tacks. About half-past eleven the signal was hove out for a general engagement, at which time the ships as they came up began firing. The French attacked at some distance the hindmost of Sir Robert Harland's division,[1] which led the van. Their fire was warmly returned by almost every ship in the fleet, as they ranged along the line ; and notwithstanding it had been extended by the chase, they were soon engaged, as the two fleets passed each other. The cannonade was very heavy, and did considerable execution on both sides. The enemy, as usual, fired chiefly at the rigging, which crippled many

---

[1] Included in Sir Robert Harland's division was the *Centaur*, seventy-four guns, crew 600 men, commanded by Captain Cosby (afterwards Admiral Cosby), uncle of Admiral Wolseley. The *Duke*, ninety-eight guns, crew 750 men (commanded by Captain Brereton), in which Admiral Wolseley was serving as junior lieutenant, was also in this division. In the division under Admiral Keppel was the *Vigilant*, sixty-four guns, crew 500, commanded by Captain Kingsmill (afterwards Sir Robert Kingsmill).

of the British ships, while Admiral Keppel continued the old way of fighting, by firing principally
at the hulls of the enemy's ships with good success.

"The action, for the short space it lasted (about
three hours), was very warm. The loss on the side
of the British was 133 killed and 373 wounded.
The French concealed their loss as much as possible; they acknowledged, however, 150 killed and
about 600 wounded. From the manner of engaging,
it is probable they lost more men than the British,
perhaps double the number.

"It was necessary to take a short time to repair
the damages, which being done, the commander-in-
chief made the signal to form the line of battle
ahead. The Red Division, commanded by Sir
Robert Harland, immediately obeyed; but the Blue
Division never came into the line during the rest
of the day, Sir Hugh Palliser alleging that his ship,
the *Formidable*, was so much disabled that he could
not obey the signal."

And Dr. Campbell remarks :—"It is evident that
a fair opportunity was lost of striking a blow against
the maritime power of France which might have
been decisive.

"It appeared, by the evidence of witnesses upon
oath, in the subsequent trials of Keppel and Palliser,
that the French, on purpose to deceive, stationed,
soon after it was dark, three of their best sailing-
ships in a line, at considerable distances from each
other, with lights, in order to have the appearance

B

of their whole fleet. This *finesse* had the intended effect; their fleet stole away in the night, and the three ships followed them at daylight in the morning.

"The British fleet was nearly in a line of battle all night, excepting the *Formidable* and some other ships of Sir Hugh Palliser's division. The men were on deck all night in every ship of the fleet, quartered at their guns, ready to renew the action in the morning; but the whole French fleet was then out of sight, excepting the three ships already mentioned, and they were also at too great a distance to be overtaken.

"The commander, discovering that the French had escaped, that many ships of his own fleet had suffered greatly in their masts and rigging, and that there was not the least prospect of overtaking the enemy before they could reach Brest, had no alternative but to bring the fleet home to be repaired. He arrived off Plymouth on the 31st of July.

"Admiral Keppel put to sea again," continues Dr. Campbell, "with the same number of ships and commanders, on the 22nd of August. The French had left Brest some days before, but instead of looking out for the British fleet, they bore away for Cape Finisterre, leaving their trade at the mercy of our fleet and privateers. Many of their merchantmen accordingly fell into the hands of the English. The British admiral continued cruising

in the bay till the 28th of October, when he returned to Portsmouth, and the French got to Brest
a few days after."

Admiral Wolseley continues:— "In 1779 Sir
Edward Hughes was again appointed to the command in India. With his flag on board the *Superb*
and ten sail of the line and a large fleet of Indiamen, I thought it a fine opportunity to forward
myself in my profession, and I applied to Sir
Edward Hughes to take me with him. He very
kindly said he could not take me into his own ship,
there being no vacancy, but that if I could get an
exchange into one of the ships going under his
command he would attend to me. I fortunately
met at this period a lieutenant who wanted to
exchange from the *Worcester*, sixty-four guns, into
the *Duke*. The exchange was effected immediately,
and I became second lieutenant of the *Worcester*,
George Talbot commander.

" Sir Edward Hughes sailed with ten sail of the
line, the *Worcester* included,[1] and several Indiamen
with troops. We went to the island of Goree, on
the coast of Guinea, in the hands of the French.
Previous to getting into Goree, I was appointed to
command a flat boat for the purpose of landing
troops, as it was Sir Edward Hughes's intention to
storm the garrison ; the French, however, beat a
parley and surrendered garrison. We afterwards

---

[1] Admiral Wolseley says :—" Five sail of the line were as an escort,
and left him on going through Channel."

touched at the Cape of Good Hope, and proceeded
from thence to Madras.

" We then went with five sail of the line (including the *Worcester*) to Bombay, and sent a small
frigate (the *Coventry*), commanded by Captain
Andrew Mitchell, who had the naval part under
his direction, and the boats of the squadron,
to Arnault (or Arnaut), a piratical state between
Surat and Bombay. I was a volunteer on this
occasion ; I also volunteered for the storming party.
The East India Company's general, whose name
was Goddard, commanded. We besieged the garrison of Arnault, and reduced it to capitulate, just
as we were about to storm it.

" From thence we proceeded to the Malabar
coast to attack Hyder Ally's squadron at Manga-
lore, consisting of one large frigate and two sloops,
which were hauled so close in that we boarded
them in the boats of the fleet. The enemy's
squadron was burnt and destroyed 18th of December 1780 ; we lost a great number of officers and
men on this occasion.

" Some time afterwards the war broke out with
Holland, and we went to attack Negapatam, which
was a Dutch settlement, October 21, 1781. It being
found necessary to have a naval battalion of 800
men, I was appointed to the battalion with 100
men from the *Worcester*; and when landed I was
appointed adjutant to the naval battalion. On
this service I was employed two or three months.

Sir Hector Munro, of the Company's service, was the general commanding in chief. We besieged Negapatam,[1] and suffered two sorties from the garrison, which we beat off. It then surrendered, and we embarked our men.

"Previous to the attack of Negapatam by the navy battalion, I commanded the barge of the *Worcester* to the attack and taking of forty sail of coasters, small vessels, out of Negapatam roads.

"On the 2nd of January 1782, Vice-Admiral Sir Edward Hughes sailed with the squadron from Negapatam to carry into execution the design he had formed for the reduction of the Dutch settlement of Trincomali, in the island of Ceylon. Here I was again landed in the navy battalion, and with the troops was sent in with Major Giles to summon Fort Ostenberg at Trincomali. In this service 450 seamen and marines were employed, out of which small force two lieutenants and twenty men were killed and forty wounded. We stormed the fort on the 11th of January. My company was the first storming party after the marines, and I was severely wounded in the trenches. Fort Ostenberg was carried, and 80,000 dollars and two sail of Dutch Indiamen, &c., fell into our hands."

Neither in the little memoir nor in the memo-

[1] Dr. Campbell says in his "Naval History" that the Dutch settlement of Negapatam surrendered in the month of November 1781. He says the squadron lost on this occasion seventeen seamen killed and twenty-seven wounded; thirteen marines killed and twenty-nine wounded.

randum from which I have been quoting does
Admiral Wolseley mention that on this occasion
he volunteered to lead the sailors sent to the
attack of this fort, and that he went in the place
of a young officer who had been recently married,
and who was previously appointed by the captain
to take the command of the party sent from the
Worcester. This circumstance, so indicative of his
generosity and courage, was told to the Admiral's
daughters, many years after, by Captain Hayes, an
old friend and comrade of their father's, who had
also served as a lieutenant on board the *Worcester*
during the war in the East Indies.

As Admiral Wolseley gives no account of the
attack, I take the following from Dr. Campbell's
notice of it in his " Naval History " :—" Trincomali,
on the island of Ceylon, was taken by assault on
the 11th of January 1782, together with two Dutch
ships, richly laden, which were in the harbour,
and several small vessels. The particulars of the
attack," continues Dr. Campbell, "we extract from
Sir Edward Hughes's official account of the capture
of the place:—' The necessary disposition was made
for the attack to begin at daylight in the morning
of the 11th, and accordingly the storming party,
composed of 450 seamen and marines, and their
officers,[1] with each flank covered by a party of
pioneers, and twenty seamen carrying the scaling-

---

[1] The number of seamen and marines mentioned by Admiral Wolseley were evidently those of the storming company only.

ladders and armed with cutlasses, with a reserve of three companies of seamen, three companies of marines, two field-pieces to support it, and followed by the Company's troops, advanced at daylight towards the fort. The sergeant's party in front, getting in at the embrasures, was immediately followed by the whole of the storming party, who soon drove the enemy from their works and possessed themselves of the fort; and all the ships and vessels in the harbour immediately surrendered.'"

Sir Edward Hughes places the killed and wounded in this assault at the number stated by Admiral Wolseley, and among those who were wounded, mentions "Lieutenant Wolseley, who commanded a company of seamen."

He makes the remark that "the enemy lost but few men," and that, when they threw down their arms, their forfeited lives were spared by that disposition to mercy which ever distinguishes Britons."

Captain Hayes told Admiral Wolseley's daughters that the garrison of the fort was a large one, and said that the fire from the walls was extremely hot. While in the trench surrounding the castle, trying to effect an entrance, Admiral Wolseley was severely wounded in the chest. The shot was fired from the castle walls, from a long, heavy gun called a *gingal*, a weapon said to have been very generally used in the East in the defence of fortresses, and which was usually loaded with very large-sized bullets and

broken pieces of lead.   Two unfortunate sailors of
Admiral Wolseley's company, who were fighting at
each side of him, were killed immediately after he
was wounded, and fell partly across him as he
lay in the trench.   In the hurry of collecting the
wounded, and getting them into the boats after the
fort was taken, Mr. Wolseley was not missed until
the party had returned to the *Worcester;* and it
was then thought that he must have been killed.

   Mr. Hayes, who was greatly attached to Mr.
Wolseley, wanted to return at once to look for
him ; but the captain, thinking it useless, would
not hear of it, as it was then almost quite dark.
Mr. Hayes sat up all night, watching anxiously
for the dawn, and then went off in the first boat
with the party who were sent to bury their fallen
comrades.   Mr. Wolseley had on this occasion a
most providential escape ; and the presence of his
friend, Captain Hayes, was the means of saving his
life.   When he was found by the party searching
for him, Mr. Wolseley was quite unconscious, and
was still lying in the long grass at the bottom of
the trench, under the two sailors who were killed
just after he had received the wound.   Excepting
Mr. Hayes, all the rest of the party were convinced
that Mr. Wolseley was dead, and only that that
officer was present, and prevented them, would have
buried him with the unfortunate men who had lost
their lives.   But, fortunately for him, Mr. Hayes,
thinking that there were still some signs of life,

insisted upon having him carried down to one of the boats, and at once took him off to the *Worcester*, where the surgeon, who at first thought the case a hopeless one, at last managed to revive him.

Admiral Wolseley does not mention this narrow escape in the memoir, and merely continues :—

"After I was wounded, I was removed, from being second lieutenant of the *Worcester*, to the *Superb* (Sir Edward Hughes's flagship), as youngest lieutenant, and was favourably mentioned in Sir E. Hughes's despatches to the Admiralty. Having put things in order in Trincomali, we sailed to Madras, and there took in rice for the army under the great Sir Eyre Coote, and went with it to Cuddalore, where the troops were in distress for provisions, being blocked up by Hyder Ally.

"This supply enabled them to retreat, and from the mastheads of the ships we saw the whole of Hyder Ally's and Tippoo Sahib's army attack our troops. The enemy's cavalry made some movements on the occasion, which brought them very near the sea-coast on a flat country, and the ships fired on them, which drove them back in confusion. Sir Eyre Coote made good his retreat to Madras, where the fleet also went."

CHAPTER II

"HITHERTO the British fleet," writes Dr. Campbell, "had continued undisturbed masters of the Indian seas ; but towards the end of the year 1781, a French squadron of considerable force arrived from Europe, under the command of M. de Suffrein, one of the ablest officers that the French marine has ever produced.[1] The views of the French Ministry in sending this squadron to India were of a nature that struck at the very root of the British dominions in Asia; the squadron was intended to co-operate with the native powers who were at war with the English, and they carried with them a large body of troops, the more effectually to answer that end."

Five great naval battles took place between the two fleets after the arrival of Admiral de Suffrein ; and in four of these Admiral Wolseley took part, as junior lieutenant, on board of Admiral Sir Edward Hughes's flag-ship, the *Superb*, of seventy-four guns. In almost all these engagements the numerical superiority was on the side of the French. Colonel

---

[1] Elsewhere the Doctor remarks that Admiral de Suffrein was "worthy of being the rival and opponent of Sir Edward Hughes"; and other writers call Suffrein "the French Nelson."

Malleson, the author of a very interesting book entitled "Final French Struggles in India," gives the names of the different ships, both French and English, and the number of guns in each vessel, that took part in these battles. He mentions that in the first action the English had "a total armament of 590 guns, while that of the French amounted to 710 guns"; and this difference of strength apparently varied but little during the course of the war.

According to Captain Brenton, R.N., author of a "Naval History of Great Britain from 1733 to 1836," besides their superiority in numbers, the French ships were better constructed, better sailers, and had larger crews than our own vessels. Writing about the state of the navy at that period, he says :— "At the close of the American war England had, according to the statement of Viscount Keppel, then First Lord of the Admiralty, one hundred sail of the line fit for active service, with a great number of frigates, sloops, and various smaller vessels ; and to man them we had 150,000 seamen, including 25,000 marines. Ships of the line at that time comprised all from one hundred guns down to those of sixty-four guns inclusive." And he adds:—"It may be adduced as a singular proof of the prowess of our seamen, that the ships of France and Spain were generally superior to those of England, both in size, weight of metal, and number of men, out-sailing them in fleets, and often in single ships, carrying their guns higher out of the water, and in all other respects better found in the material of war, particularly in the article of gunpowder."

The British fleet having returned to Madras, Admiral Wolseley says :—"Soon afterwards we heard of the French admiral (Admiral Suffrein) coming to attack the English with ten sail of the line and a body of troops, conjointly with Hyder Ally, to drive the English, if possible, out of the Carnatic. The fleet under Sir Edward Hughes, being nine sail of the line, got ready to receive Admiral Suffrein. He came in sight with his fleet, and was to windward of the English fleet. After a close survey of the latter, he bore up with the intention of attacking Trincomali ; and as soon as we found we could weather him, we weighed and gave him chase. This happened late in the evening, and in the night-time some of the English frigates engaged with two ships *armées en flûte*, which were captured."

As Admiral Wolseley says very little about the different battles fought at this time between the French and English fleets, I take some extracts concerning them from the accounts given by Dr. Campbell and Colonel Malleson, as both these authors mention some interesting details omitted in the little memoir from which I have just been quoting.

The following description of the arrival of Admiral de Suffrein in Madras roads, and the subsequent engagement between the two fleets, is thus given by Dr. Campbell :—"On the 15th of February 1782 M. de Suffrein appeared in the offing with eleven sail of the line. The English admiral had only nine two-decked ships, one of which carried but fifty guns ; he, however, prepared for an engagement by placing his ships in the most advantageous position, with springs on their cables, so that they and the numerous shipping which lay further in the road might be defended with the greatest prospect of a successful issue to the contest. M. de Suffrein, however, did not think proper to attack them in this position, but stood out of the bay to the southward ; he was immediately pursued by Sir Edward Hughes, with the hope of being able to cut off some of the numerous transports which were under the protection of the enemy's fleet. He succeeded in capturing several of them, and the French admiral, apprehensive that more would be taken, bore down with all the sail he could carry. No action, however, took place on the 16th, and the first meeting of the hostile squadrons was on the 17th of February, when a severe engagement ensued."

Admiral Wolseley says :—"We found by a change of wind that we were to leeward of the French fleet, who bore down and attacked. They were eleven sail of line, and we were but nine. Admiral Suffrein, with his two supporters, came down on and attacked the *Superb*."

Dr. Campbell continues :—"About four o'clock in

the afternoon M. de Suffrein was enabled by a favourable change of wind to bring his whole force against the centre and rear of the British, which were nearly becalmed, and at some distance from their van ; thus five ships of our squadron were exposed to the attack of the whole French fleet. This unequal contest was maintained with great spirit and vigour till about six o'clock, when a favourable breeze reached the other part of the British fleet, and enabled them to come up to the assistance of the centre and the rear.   The enemy, now that the battle was put upon a more equal footing, did not long continue it ; but, having suffered very severely, he hauled his wind and stood off to the north-east.   M. de Suffrein, in this engagement, had directed his principal attack against two of the British fleet, the *Superb* and the *Exeter ;* the latter at one time stood singly the fire of five ships."

"At seven o'clock, when it was dark," Colonel Malleson remarks, "the combat ceased as if by mutual consent ;" and Admiral Wolseley mentions that "the engagement lasted until the sea-breeze set in and both fleets were separated."   He continues :—" In this action, which occurred in Madras roads, the ships, especially the *Superb* and the *Exeter*, commanded by Sir Richard King, were so much injured that Sir E. Hughes determined to proceed to Trincomali, as the only proper place to refit them, where he arrived on the 24th."

Writing on the subject of the battle fought on the 17th of February 1782, Dr. Campbell says:—" Indecisive as this engagement was, its consequences were of the greatest importance to the stability of the British empire in India. The French had been for years preparing this armament at a vast expense, and had formed the most flattering prospects of its success; its arrival in India was regarded by the enemies of the British Government in that quarter as the final period of our power on the coast of Coromandel. Upon its assistance Hyder Ally had formed the strongest hopes of our expulsion, and the French themselves came in full confidence of a complete victory. We can scarcely regard that as a drawn battle which was the means of disappointing these mighty expectations, and of defeating a project which threatened our political existence in India. The Governor-General and Council of Bengal, in their letter of congratulation to Sir Edward Hughes on this occasion, make use of the following forcible expressions, which, when we consider their rank, and the opportunities they had of judging of the extent of the danger which threatened them, will convey a strong idea of the value of our admiral's service :—'We regard,' say they, 'your action with the French fleet as the crisis of our fate in the Carnatic, and in the result of it we see that province relieved and preserved, and the permanency fo the British power in India firmly established.'"

Admiral Wolseley continues :—" The necessary
repairs having been completed with the utmost
expedition, Sir Edward Hughes sailed for Trincomali on the 4th of March. On the 12th we
anchored with the squadron in Madras road, without having seen or heard anything of the enemy.
Sir Edward Hughes, being very weakly manned,
applied for some Europeans from Madras, and the
98th Regiment, commanded by General Sir William
Meadowes, volunteered for the service. Colonel
Fullerton was the lieutenant-colonel.

" On the 30th, we being on our way back to
Trincomali with the reinforcement of troops and
a supply of military stores for the garrison, we
were joined by the *Sultan*, of seventy-four guns,
and the *Magnanime*, of sixty-four guns, from England. These ships, having had a tedious and bad
passage, were extremely sickly, and the crews much
reduced by the scurvy."

Dr. Campbell remarks :—" As Sir Edward had on
board the squadron a reinforcement of troops for
the garrison of Trincomali and a quantity of military stores, he judged it most advantageous for the
public service, especially as he knew the enemy's
squadron was to the southward, not to return to
Madras to land the sick of the two ships, but to
proceed directly for Trincomali, 'without,' to use
his own words, 'either seeking or avoiding the
enemy.' On the 6th of April the squadron fell
in with a French ship, which they chased on shore

and burnt near Tranquebar, but the officers and men escaped, and carried off with them despatches for their commanders-in-chief by sea and land.

"Sir Edward Hughes's principal object was to protect a valuable convoy which was coming from England, and part of which had put into Morebat Bay some time before. M. de Suffrein was apprized of the approach and the importance of this convoy, and he determined to use his utmost endeavours to intercept it before its union with the English fleet. On the 8th of April the hostile fleets came in sight of each other, and they continued in sight at nearly the same distance asunder and in the same relative position for three days, when Sir Edward Hughes, being within fifteen leagues of Trincomali, stood directly for that port. By changing his course, in order to reach the place of his destination, he unavoidably gave the enemy an opportunity of gaining the wind of him; of this M. de Suffrein immediately took advantage, and on the morning of the 12th they were in close pursuit of the British squadron.

"It was absolutely necessary now to prepare for battle; for the French ships, being much cleaner in their hulls and better found in their rigging, were gaining very fast on the rear. The British fleet were placed under most disadvantageous circumstances, in every point of view, for battle; close in pursuit of them was a very superior enemy, coming on with a favourable wind; on every other side of

c

them was a rocky and dangerous coast. They had, however, no choice but to fight, and to fight in that manner which the French admiral might think would be most advantageous to himself. Although everything was so very favourable to the enemy, yet he still seemed very undetermined, either whether he should engage or not, or at least respecting the manner in which he would make the attack; for he continued making alterations in his line and in the position of his fleet for nearly three hours."

Colonel Malleson says, in his account of this battle, that Suffrein began the action about half-past twelve o'clock. Dr. Campbell continues :—
" His plan, when determined upon, was rather of a novel nature, and seemed to threaten, if carried into full and successful execution, the complete destruction of the British squadron. He divided his own fleet into two parts. One division, consisting of five sail, bore down on the van of the British; the other division, consisting of seven ships of the line, himself leading, directed their attack on the *Superb*, which was in the centre of the British line, and upon the *Monmouth*, which was ahead, and the *Monarch*, which was astern of her. The *Superb*, however, was the principal object against which the French admiral's ship and his second, both seventy-fours, poured a most dreadful cannonade, within pistol-shot. In ten minutes' time the English ship had returned the fire, in such a superior style that M. de

Suffrein shot ahead, and permitted some other vessels of his squadron to occupy his position while he proceeded to the attack of the *Monmouth*; by this manœuvre the British centre was laid open to several of the enemy's fleet, who bore down and fired with great impetuosity.

"At three o'clock the *Monmouth* was so much damaged that she was compelled to quit the line. While the battle was thus going on, the British fleet was gradually drawing nearer the shore; Sir Edward Hughes, therefore, being apprehensive that they would either get entangled with it or drop into shallow water, made the signal for them to wear, still continuing to engage the enemy." And the battle went on until, as Colonel Malleson states in his account, "suddenly, at six o'clock, a tremendous storm burst upon both fleets, enveloping them in darkness, and forcing them close to a lee shore, and to pay attention to their own safety." Dr. Campbell says :—"It was nearly dark when the French frigate, *La Fixe*, of forty guns, by some mistake, fell on board the *Isis*, and on perceiving the force of that vessel, struck her flag to her; the darkness of the night, however, preventing the latter from immediately taking possession of her prize, she hoisted her colours again and made her escape."

Admiral Wolseley says of this battle:—"This was a very severe action, and the loss in both fleets was considerable. No captures, however, were made on either side; although one of the French ships had struck her colours, and as the English were too weak to take possession before a change of wind, consequently she escaped.

"The *Monmouth*, Captain James Alms, was dismasted, and several other English ships were very much injured. The French admiral fell to leeward of us, and his ship, the *Héros*, was on fire; it was, however, at last extinguished. In the *Superb* we had a disastrous explosion, which put one hundred and fifty men *hors-de-combat;* two lieutenants and the master, with two of the military officers, were killed on this occasion."

Dr. Campbell remarks that, in the battle fought on the 12th of April, "of the English fleet, the *Superb* and *Monmouth* suffered most." And he adds:—"As soon as the *Monmouth* was fitted with jury-masts, so as to be able to keep up with the rest of the fleet, the British admiral weighed anchor, and proceeded to Trincomali Bay; the French repairing to Batacola, a Dutch port in the island of Ceylon, about twenty leagues to the south of the former place."

"On the 23rd of June 1782," continues Admiral Wolseley, "Sir Edward Hughes, having refitted his ships, and taken on board the recovered men, sailed from Trincomali in quest of the French; the next day he anchored with the squadron in Negapatam road. At this place we were informed that the enemy were at anchor off Cuddalore, and that they had captured the *Resolution* and *Raikes*, armed transports laden with stores and ammunition, on their passage to Trincomali. The afternoon of the 5th July the enemy's squadron appeared off Negapatam, consisting of eighteen sail."

Admiral Wolseley then briefly mentions that " on the 6th of July 1782 an action took place between the two fleets." And he adds :—" In this action fell Captain Dunbar Maclellan, of the *Superb*."

Following my previous plan, I now turn to Dr. Campbell's and Colonel Malleson's accounts for some details of the battle. The first-mentioned writer says that on the arrival of the fleet at Negapatam, Sir Edward heard that the French were at Cuddalore, "which place had surrendered to their land forces."

" On the 20th of June," writes Colonel Malleson, " the French fleet arrived at Cuddalore,[1] and Suffrein, intending to make a dash at Negapatam, embarked on board his transports, besides siege materials, 1200 men of the line, 400 levies of the islands, two companies of artillery, and 800 sepoys. He was on the point of sailing when intelligence reached him that the English fleet, emerging from Trincomali, had passed Cuddalore, and was bearing up northward in the direction of the place which he had hoped to surprise.

" Disappointed, but still determined, Suffrein at

---

[1] Colonel Malleson, who probably takes his account of these events from some French writer, calls this place "Kandaléur;" but as Admiral Wolseley and Dr. Campbell both speak of it as "Cuddalore," I have substituted the latter name in my extract.

once set sail in pursuit of the enemy. Coming in sight of Negapatam on the 5th July, he beheld the English fleet lying at anchor in the roadstead. Determined at all hazards to force on an action, Suffrein signalled to clear decks and to be ready to anchor. His own ship, the *Héros*, was leading, when, at three o'clock, a sudden squall caused the *Ajax*, which was following, the loss of her main and mizzen topmasts. These, and other damages almost as serious, forced her to drop out of line. The squall, settling into a steady breeze, gave the English admiral the advantage of the wind. He accordingly weighed anchor and stood out to sea. That night the two fleets anchored within two cannon-shots of each other." According to Admiral Wolseley, and Dr. Campbell also, the French fleet consisted of eighteen vessels. Colonel Malleson speaks of only sixteen, but the former number is doubtless correctly given as the strength of the enemy. Our own fleet consisted, according to Colonel Malleson, of "eleven line-of-battle ships (carrying 746 guns) and one frigate."

On the morning of the 6th July, Colonel Malleson says, "the English admiral determined to use his advantage of the wind and to force on an engagement. At ten minutes past seven, then, he formed his line ahead, and signalled to his captains that each ship should bear down as directly as possible upon her opponent and endeavour to bring her to close action."

Dr. Campbell says :—"Some time before the British ships had reached the respective positions which, by signal, they were directed to take, the enemy had commenced firing; in this respect following their accustomed practice of endeavouring to disable our vessels as they bore down from windward upon them. The British, however, did not return the fire till they had nearly reached the position they meant to occupy; then they began a heavy and well-directed cannonade. Soon after noon the action was general from van to rear." Colonel Malleson says :—"The French commodore's ship, the *Héros*, seventy-four, and the English admiral's ship, the *Superb*, seventy-four, engaged in an almost hand-to-hand encounter."

"The fire of the British," continues Dr. Campbell, "was so effectual that in a very short time one vessel of the enemy was obliged to draw out of the line, another had lost her mainmast, and all of them were evidently much disabled, both in their hulls and rigging. Everything seemed now to promise that this battle would be more decisive than the former ones, and that it would terminate in the defeat of the French, when unfortunately, the wind, which frequently in these latitudes changes at noon, veered round; many of the British ships in the van and the rear were taken aback and thrown into confusion, being obliged by the change of wind to draw out of the line. Most of our ships, which were thus thrown into confusion from this cause, had suffered considerably in their rigging, so that they could not be easily and speedily manœuvred in such a manner as to regain their position ; those, however, which had suffered comparatively little damage, and that composed the British rear, soon came to the wind and the larboard tack, and recommenced the action.

"As it was of the utmost importance to remedy the confusion into which the British fleet had been thrown by this unexpected change of wind, Sir Edward Hughes hauled down the signal for the line, and made the signal for the ships to wear, with an intention of giving chase to the enemy, who, profiting by the same circumstance which had been so adverse to our squadron, had commenced their flight. But at this time the British admiral perceived that some of his own ships were so much disabled that they could neither give chase nor continue the fight if they could have come up with the enemy; while the *Eagle*, another of his squadron, having by the change of wind been carried very near the enemy, was in danger of being cut off by them; he was, therefore, compelled to abandon his design of giving chase, and at half-past five o'clock anchored between Negapatam and Najore. The French stood in shore, and when they had neared it, collected their squadron in a close body, in such a manner and position as to be safe from the attack of the British.

"Thus the fleets continued all that night, each employed in repairing the damages they had sustained.

Sir Edward Hughes soon found that his vessels had suffered so much in their masts and rigging that the further pursuit of the enemy would be impossible ; while the French fleet having, as usual, suffered much more in their hulls than in their masts and rigging, were enabled the next morning, to the mortification of their opponents, to return to Cuddalore road ; the disabled ships forming the van, and those which had suffered comparatively little, with the frigates, covering their retreat.

" During this engagement, the *Sévère*, one of the French squadron, had fallen on board the *Sultan*, at the time when the sudden change of wind took place, and struck her colours as soon as she perceived her situation. The captain of the *Sultan* was prevented from taking possession of her by his anxiety to obey the signal, just then thrown out, of wearing and joining the admiral ; the *Sévère* took advantage of this circumstance, and, being separated from the *Sultan* by the manœuvre of that vessel in the act of wearing, she hoisted her colours again, or, as some maintain, even without displaying any colours, she poured a broadside into the British ship. In consequence of this strange conduct, Sir Edward Hughes, after the engagement was over, sent a flag of truce to M. de Suffrein, demanding the *Sévère* as a lawful prize. To this demand the French admiral sent an evasive answer ; denying, however, that the colours had been actually struck, but maintaining that they had

been shot away by accident. In this action, which, like the preceding one, was obstinate, well fought, but indecisive, the British had 77 killed and 233 wounded; the loss of the enemy was 178 killed and 601 wounded."

In reference to the battle just described, Dr. Campbell gives some extracts from Sir Edward Hughes's official account. In it the admiral says :—
" I am extremely happy to inform their lordships that in this engagement his Majesty's squadron, under my command, gained a decided superiority over that of the enemy; and had not the wind shifted, and thrown his Majesty's squadron out of the action, at the very time when some of the enemy's ships had broken their line and were running away, and others of them greatly disabled, I have good reason to believe it would have ended in the capture of several of their line - of - battle ships."

"The British admiral," continues Dr. Campbell, "finding it impossible to pursue the enemy, after the engagement, without a supply of spars and cordage, and the ammunition of the squadron, as well as its provisions, being nearly exhausted, was obliged to proceed with his ships to Madras roads, the only place where he could obtain a supply of the necessaries which he wanted. Sir Edward arrived at Madras on the 20th of July, and immediately exerted himself, with his usual zeal and activity, to put the squadron in a condition for service."

Colonel Malleson states that while the fleet was at Madras the admiral "was joined by the *Sceptre* and the *San Carlos*." And he says:—"The damages which many of his ships had sustained were considerable, and he was forced to make extraordinary exertions to repair them. It had occurred to him that the French commander might take advantage of the state of his vessels, and the gain of a fortnight's time, to make an attempt on Trincomali. To guard as much as possible against such an attempt, he despatched the *Monmouth* and the *Sceptre*, with supplies of men and ammunition, to that place." Colonel Malleson continues:—"His anxiety on the subject was soon roused, however, to a greater extent than ever.

"When the French frigate *Bellona* had fought an indecisive action with the *Coventry* off Batacola, the combating vessels approached sufficiently near to that place to enable the captain of the latter ship to see the whole French fleet at anchor. He at once crowded on sail, to carry the news quickly to Madras. He reached Madras in the middle of August, and gave the first intimation to Sir E. Hughes of the dangerous proximity to Trincomali of his enemy. Sir Edward used all the despatch possible to hasten his departure for Ceylon. At length he set out, but, delayed by contrary winds, he arrived before Trincomali only to see the French flag flying on all the forts and the French fleet at anchor in the bay. Trincomali had capitulated on the 31st August. It was occupied by the French on the 1st September. On the 2nd the fleet of Sir Edward Hughes appeared in sight of the place."

Dr. Campbell states that "M. de Suffrein had been reinforced by the *Illustre*, a ship of seventy-four guns; the *St. Michael*, of sixty-four; and the *Elizabeth*, of fifty, a ship formerly belonging to the East India Company, and his squadron had also received a supply of necessaries by a convoy of transports from Europe." And Colonel Malleson mentions that "the French ships carried in all 1038 guns, and the English ships only 976 guns."

On the morning of the 3rd September, according to Colonel Malleson, Suffrein held a council of war composed of the captains of his different vessels, most of whom "urged upon the commodore the advisability of resting upon his laurels." Colonel Malleson continues :—" Before giving a decisive answer to his peace-pleading captains, Suffrein determined to ascertain the number of the enemy's vessels. He accordingly signalled to the frigate *Bellona* to reconnoitre. The *Bellona* in a very short space of time signalled back that there were twelve English ships. This decided Suffrein, as he had fourteen.

"The fact is," Colonel Malleson remarks, "that Suffrein saw, though his captains could not or would not see, that a grand opportunity, possibly the last, now offered to strike a decisive blow for dominion in Southern India. Could he but destroy, or effectually disable, the fleet of Sir Edward Hughes, everything was still possible. Bussy was on the point of arriving; Haidar Ali still lived, threatening the English possessions all round Madras; the attenuated English army, deprived of its fleet, would be unable to keep the field; and there was nothing to prevent the victorious French fleet from sailing with the monsoon wind to Madras and crushing out the domination of the English in the countries south of the river Krishna. There was the one obstacle offered by the twelve ships of Sir Edward Hughes; and Suffrein had fourteen."

However, to return to the events of that memorable day, the 3rd of September 1782, Colonel Malleson continues:—"Decided by the signal from the *Bellona* to fight, Suffrein weighed anchor and stood out towards his enemy." "Sir Edward Hughes, on his part," writes Dr. Campbell, "was equally ready and desirous of fighting; but in order that he might engage to more advantage, and if possible render the battle more decisive than the former ones, he endeavoured to draw the enemy after him as far as possible from Trincomali.

"M. de Suffrein at first followed with great alacrity, his fleet consisting of fourteen sail of the line, three frigates, and a fire-ship. When, however, he had made a considerable offing, he appeared to waver in his resolution, at one time seeming disposed to come to action, and at another time bringing to, or edging down towards the shore

again." This apparent irresolution was probably
caused by the conduct of some of the commanders
of Admiral Suffrein's vessels; for, according to
Colonel Malleson, "as he (Suffrein) approached he
signalled to form line in prearranged order. This
signal, though repeated again and again, was so
badly executed by some of the malcontent captains
that it appeared to the English as if their enemy
was about, after all, to decline an engagement."

"At length, about noon," continues Dr. Campbell,
"he manœuvred in such a manner that there could
not remain any doubt that he had made up his
mind to engage; he probably was led to this resolution by observing that the *Worcester*, the rear
ship of the British squadron, had fallen considerably
behind. On her, therefore, two of the French fleet
fell with great fury; but she fought with so much
bravery, and was manœuvred at the same time
with so much skill, that the *Monmouth*, which was
directly ahead of her, had time to bear down to
her assistance. While this was going on, five of
the enemy's ships, pushing on under a crowd of sail
and in a compact body, fell on the *Exeter* and
the *Isis*, the two headmost ships of the British
squadron. For some time these vessels fought
against this great superiority of force, till the
former, being much disabled, was compelled to
draw out of the line; the enemy, upon this, tacked,
and fired upon the whole of our van, as they passed
them in succession."

"But the most desperate engagement was that between the centres of the hostile fleets ; especially between the *Superb* and *Héros*, the ships of the two commanders." Colonel Malleson says:—"Whilst this murderous hand-to-hand conflict was going on in the centre, the two extremities continued pounding at each other at long distances. In this the French had somewhat the advantage;" although, as he says, "the *Consulante*, a 40-gun frigate, which had been brought into action, lost her captain ; the *Vengeur*, having fired away all her ammunition, withdrew from the line, and caught fire, with difficulty extinguished ; and the remainder of the squadron continued to fire without order, and at long distances, notwithstanding that the signal for close action was still flying on the commodore's ship.

"At four o'clock in the afternoon, the fight having then lasted one hour and a half, the situation of the French commodore had become extremely critical. The *Ajax* had been so riddled as to be able to retire only with the greatest difficulty. The *Héros*, the *Illustre*, and the *Brillant* had to bear unsupported the weight of the concentrated fire of the centre division of the English fleet. At four o'clock the *Artésien* came to the commodore's rescue ; but even then the odds were too great. About five o'clock the mainmast, the fore-topmast, and the mizzen-topmast of the *Héros* came down with a tremendous crash. The hurrahs of the English first showed Suffrein that they thought he had struck

his flag. Not for long did they remain under this
delusion. Rushing on the poop, Suffrein cried with
a voice that sounded above the roar of the combat,
'Bring flags; bring up all the white flags that
are below and cover my ship with them.' These
words," continues Colonel Malleson, "inspired his
men with renewed energy. The contest continued
with greater fury than ever. The *Burford*, the
Sultan, and the *Superb* had already felt, and now
felt again, its effects. Hope was beginning to rise
among the French when it was whispered to
Suffrein that he had already expended 1800 rounds
of shot, and that his ammunition was exhausted.
Powder, however, remained, and with powder alone
he continued to fire, so as to delude the enemy."

The French were, however, as Dr. Campbell
remarks, "a second time befriended and saved by
a sudden change of the wind." And "suddenly, at
half-past five, the wind shifted from the south-west
to the east-south-east. This enabled the vanguard
of the French fleet to come to the aid of and to
cover its centre;" and "as soon as the wind
changed, Sir Edward Hughes had no alternative
but to throw out the signal for his ships to wear."
"But on resuming their position," writes Colonel
Malleson, "they had no longer the hardly pressed
ships of the French centre to encounter, but those
of the vanguard, which till then had only engaged
at a distance and were comparatively fresh.

"The battle then re-engaged. But now it was

the turn of the French. The *Hero* lost her main-mast at twenty minutes past six, and her mizzen-mast soon after. The main-topmast of the *Worcester* was shot away about the same time. At last night fell, and the engagement ceased." And it is stated by Dr. Campbell that "about seven o'clock the French steered away close to the wind, to the southward, receiving a galling fire from the British rear, which they passed ; " and he adds that it was quite impossible for Sir Edward Hughes to attempt to follow them, as "the *Superb*, *Burford*, *Eagle*, and *Monmouth* were completely disabled, and the rest of his fleet had suffered also in a greater or less degree."

Colonel Malleson says in his account that "both fleets remained all night near the scene of action. The next morning that of the French entered the harbour of Trincomali ; the English set sail for Madras." And Dr. Campbell mentions that "in entering Trincomali Bay, either from the disabled state of the ship, from negligence and want of skill, or from the confusion in which the French were, the *Orient*, of seventy-four guns, ran on shore and was lost.

" The loss of the British," the Doctor remarks, "was not nearly so great in this engagement as might have been supposed ; there were only 51 killed and 283 wounded. On board of the French fleet the killed amounted to 412, and the wounded to 676 ; the *Héros*, Admiral Suffrein's ship, lost

140 killed and 240 wounded, out of her crew of
1200 men. He was so much dissatisfied with the
conduct of some of his captains that six of them
were broke, and sent under arrest to the Mauritius."
This is borne out also by Colonel Malleson, who
makes the remark, "That the majority of the
French captains behaved disgracefully was broadly
asserted by Suffrein ; " and he states that Suffrein,
writing to a friend on the 14th, after the battle, in
a letter which was some months later published in
the *Gazette de France*, alluding to the excellent
conduct of the captain of the *Illustre*, M. de
Bruyères de Chalabre, used this expression : "No
one could have borne himself better than he did ;
if all had done like him, we should have been
masters of India for ever."

Colonel Malleson, evidently, fully agrees with
the French admiral in this, as he says :—" There
can scarcely be a doubt that if all had fought like
the captain of the *Illustre* he would have mastered
Southern India." However, be this as it may, the
great sea-fight off Trincomali resulted in another
drawn battle. But that it was a well-fought one
on the part of our brave sailors, both officers and
men, it is surely unnecessary to add. And, as Dr.
Campbell justly remarks, "though in the course
of less than twelve months Sir Edward Hughes
was four times severely engaged with a force considerably superior to his own in numbers, and commanded by an officer of as great skill and courage

as any whom his nation has ever produced, yet he maintained the honour of the British character for naval pre-eminence unsullied ; and if he gained no decisive victories, or signalised himself by any extensive defeat of the enemy, the services which he performed for his country were substantial rather than splendid, and solid rather than brilliant."

And to these remarks of Dr. Campbell's it may be added, that the importance of these four battles to British interests, and to the maintenance of our power in India, can scarcely be overrated ; and that this was the opinion of the Governor-General and Council of Bengal is shown by the extract taken by Dr. Campbell from the letter addressed by them to Sir Edward Hughes.

CHAPTER III

In all these four battles fought in the year 1782, which, under Providence, were the means of preserving the Empire of India to the English, Admiral Wolseley took his part as lieutenant on board Sir Edward Hughes's flag-ship, the *Superb*; and this vessel, as shown by the accounts given by Dr. Campbell and Colonel Malleson, invariably bore the full brunt of the attack, being generally singled out and attacked by Suffrein himself. These four engagements, the first on the 17th of February, the second on the 12th of April, the third on the 6th of July, and the fourth on the 3rd of September, with the former battle fought against the French by the English fleet under Lord Keppel and Sir Hugh Palliser on the 17th July 1778, made five general actions, in which Admiral Wolseley took part during the time he was a lieutenant.

Of the last engagement, so fully described by Colonel Malleson, Admiral Wolseley briefly says in his memoir :—" On the 3rd of September 1782, Sir Edward Hughes being again near Trincomali, another action took place between him and Suffrein. Two of the French ships fell furiously on the *Worcester*, but she made so brave a resistance, and being timely supported by the *Monmouth*, her second ahead, the attack of the French failed entirely on that side. Captains Watt of the *Sultan*, Wood of the *Worcester*, and Lumley of the *Isis* lost their lives by this action."

He continues :—" I was then made master and commander of the *Combustion*, and acting-captain of the *Worcester* on Captain Wood's being wounded. I took the *Worcester* into Madras roads, and on poor Captain Wood's dying at Madras I was made post-captain into the *Coventry*, twenty-eight guns, from the *Combustion*.

" In a short time, the monsoon having set in, and the French having gone for refuge from it to the island of Andaman and the adjacent coast about Achin Head, Sir Edward Hughes thought it necessary, to avoid the monsoon, to go to Bombay, and left the *Coventry* and a 32-gun frigate commanded by Sir Erasmus Gore to cruise in the Bay of Bengal for a short time, to look out for the arrival of some of our Indiamen that were expected. I went to Mirachapatam and Ganjam in the *Coventry*. I was under weigh at night going into Ganjam roads, with scarcely any wind or steerage way, when, on the haze clearing off a little, I saw two ships which we supposed to be the Indiamen, but they proved to be the French fleet. Captain Gore, in the frigate, was on the outside of the *Coventry*, with a little wind. All my efforts to get the *Coventry* off were ineffectual, and I was taken prisoner.

"Admiral Suffrein asked me to dinner, and put me on board the *Flamand*, commanded by Captain de Silver, as he spoke English; and I was taken into Trincomali, where I had leave from Admiral Suffrein to remain some time, and was given my choice of going either to the Mauritius or to Hyder Ally.

"I preferred going to the Mauritius, and soon sailed in a transport to the Isle de France, from whence, in a few days, I was, at my own request, sent to the Isle de Bourbon, where a number of officers, both of the King's and India Company's troops, were prisoners of war. Amongst them were a general officer of the Company's service and his secretary, also three captains of Indiamen, Captain Par of the navy, and many others. I remained at the Isle de Bourbon, as happy as I could be under such circumstances, for eight months. In the year 1783 peace was declared, and we were consequently all liberated."

Colonel Malleson says :—"The war was terminated by the peace known in history as the Treaty of Versailles, and the struggle ended in the triumph of England. Had it been otherwise, Madras and all southern India," he continues, "would have passed over to the French." And he adds, a few pages farther on :—"By the interval of nine years which elapsed between the signature of the Treaty of Versailles and the outbreak of the War of the Revolution, the English profited to fix their domination on a basis so substantial as to be proof against further direct hostility on the part of their great rival."

After his liberation Admiral Wolseley continues :—" Two captains of Indiamen, Captain Par and I, went in a small French transport to the Cape of Good Hope, and were going into False Bay when a strong south-easter came on. We English knew very well what would be the consequence, and we wanted the Frenchmen to go on to St. Helena, instead of stopping at the Cape. The south-easter blew away almost all his sails, and from his not having taken proper precautions, he got so far to leeward that he was obliged to do as we wished, not being able to get in to the Cape, as we had foreseen. We had a passage of ten days before we arrived at St. Helena. Here we met the *Queen*, East Indiaman, Captain Douglas, about to sail for England, who very kindly took us all on board, and after a passage of eight weeks we arrived at Plymouth. On going up to London directly afterwards to report our arrival, there was such a deep fall of snow it was found necessary to have six horses to draw the coach. Some time about that period the court-martial came on respecting the loss of the *Coventry*.[1]

" I then went to Ireland to see my mother and other relations ; this was in 1783 ; and in 1785 I was appointed captain of the *Trusty*, a new 50-gun ship,

---

[1] At this court-martial Captain Wolseley was honourably acquitted.

and I fitted her out for Commodore Philipps Cosby
(my uncle), who was appointed to the command in
the Mediterranean. It was usual on occasions of
this kind, when a ship was ready to go out from
Spithead, to make the signal for assistance, each
ship then afloat sending their boat to be of any
service. Amongst the number of those boats was
the *Hebe's* boat, with the Duke of Clarence (his late
Majesty William IV.) as midshipman attending.
He came up the gangway, pulled off his hat to me,
and asked if there were any orders ; I replied that
the boats were towing the ship, and that there were
no further commands. The Duke's boat laid hold
of the tow rope. Full twenty years after that I met
his Royal Highness at Bath, and he recalled the
whole circumstance to my recollection on the
occasion in a very flattering manner."

There was, however, rather an amusing incident
connected with Admiral Wolseley's first meeting
with the Duke of Clarence, which may have had
something to do with his Royal Highness's recollection of it. When the towing rope was first
thrown to the crew of the boat commanded by the
Duke of Clarence it fell short and went into the
water, and Captain Wolseley, who was leaning over
the side of the ship watching the proceedings, on
seeing a young midshipman sitting quietly in the
stern of the boat and not making the slightest
attempt to assist the men in catching the rope,
called out to him, " Hullo, you young monkey,

why don't you lend a hand with that rope?" To which very unceremoniously expressed demand the Duke instantly replied, "Ay, ay, sir!" and forthwith began to assist the men in hauling it in.

From 1785 till 1789 Admiral Wolseley was captain of the *Trusty*, his uncle Commodore Cosby's flag-ship, and he continues:—"We sailed in September to Gibraltar, then commanded by General Elliot, afterwards Lord Heathfield. We remained four years at the different ports in the Mediterranean, and spent a pleasant time. At one period we took the young Duke of Bedford from Nice to Leghorn. I returned in command of the *Trusty*, with Admiral Cosby's flag, to England, and was paid off in 1789.

"In the year 1792, Admiral Cosby having the command of Plymouth, I was appointed captain of the *Lowestoffe* frigate, thirty-two guns. It was then peace, but the revolutionary war broke out very early in 1793, and I was sent twice into St. George's Channel to protect the Irish convoys, and was ordered by the Admiralty to get the *Lowestoffe* up off the docks of Liverpool. From thence I sailed with about 200 seamen, and collected 300 sail of the convoy in the Irish Channel, with the intention of going with them round the Land's End, but the wind came on to blow very hard from the southwest, and I was obliged to go into Milford Haven for shelter of the convoy. In consequence of having the typhus fever on board, I had the ship fumigated here. Sir John Gore, late admiral, was my second lieutenant on board the *Lowestoffe*.

" Three or four days afterwards I got out of Milford Haven, and sailed round the Land's End, with all the convoy safe. Having been so successful in this business, the Admiralty sent me again upon the same service to the Irish Channel, to convoy the linen ships, &c., round, in which we also succeeded.

"Lord Hood was then going to the Mediterranean with ten sail of the line. Admiral Cosby being appointed third in command of these ships, the *Lowestoffe* was taken as repeating frigate to the third division; and I sailed with the fleet from Spithead. As soon as we were down Channel, clear of the Lizard, Lord Hood made my signal to go to the southward. This was intended as a compliment.

" Lord Hood took the fleet to Gibraltar. I kept the *Lowestoffe* close to the French coast in the bay, until we began to get short of water. I retook on this occasion an English merchantman, and sent her into port. I then opened Bay orders, and sailed to Gibraltar, where I joined Lord Hood and the fleet. On this service I remained with Lord Hood two or three years, and was at the taking of Toulon and Corsica."

As Admiral Wolseley merely mentions that he was present at Toulon, and gives no details of the various engagements in Corsica in which he took part, I therefore take some extracts concerning these events from the interesting accounts given by the well-known naval historians, Mr. James and Captain Brenton.

The last-mentioned author says:—"The command of the British squadron in the Mediterranean, on the peace establishment, was held by Vice-Admiral Cosby, whose flag was in the *Trusty*, of fifty guns ; he had under his orders a small squadron, consisting of six frigates and three sloops of war.

"This force was intended chiefly as a check to the Barbary powers, and to guard against the machinations of France and Spain in the south of Europe.

"It was not till the month of April 1793 that a squadron could be got ready, on the war establishment, to proceed to that part of the world." Rear-Admiral Gell sailed in the beginning of the month, with a fleet consisting of six vessels, besides his flag-ship; and having arrived at Gibraltar, continues Captain Brenton, he "was speedily reinforced by six sail of the line and two frigates, which sailed in the month of May, under the command of Vice-Admiral Hotham ; and on the 22nd of May, Lord Viscount Hood, with the third division, sailed from Spithead, to assume the chief command, and to commence the most active operations against the Republic of France. His lordship had his flag in the *Victory*, and now counted twenty sail of the line under his orders."

Lord Hood, on his arrival in the Mediterranean,
took his station off Toulon, where, at that time,
both in the town itself and in the large fleet in the
harbour, were to be found many Royalists, strongly
opposed to the Republican Government. "This
spirit of disaffection," writes Mr. James, "existed
not only to a partial extent in the fleet, but very
generally throughout the whole of the southern
provinces; and the inhabitants, for their alleged
disloyalty, were either feeling or momentarily
dreading the full weight of the Republican rage."
Such being the position of affairs, Mr. James states
that "on the 23rd of August two commissioners
came off to the *Victory*, Lord Hood's flag-ship, and
represented themselves to be charged with full
powers from the sections of the departments in
which Marseilles was situated to treat for peace,
expressly stating that the leading object of their
negotiation was to effect the re-establishment of
a monarchical government in France. They expected, they said, the immediate arrival of deputies,
similarly authorised, from the section of the department of the Var, of which Toulon was the principal
town.

"Lord Hood pledged himself that if the standard
of royalty was hoisted, the ships in Toulon dis-
mantled, and the harbour and forts were placed
provisionally at his disposal, so as to admit of
egress and regress to the British fleet, the people
of Provence should have all the assistance and

support which that fleet could afford ; that a peace upon just, liberal, and honourable principles was the sole object of the treaty ; and that on such an event taking place the port of Toulon, its batteries and shipping, with the stores of every kind, as particularised in a schedule to be drawn up, should be restored to France." (This treaty, Captain Brenton states, was signed on board the *Victory* on the 28th of August 1793.) Mr. James continues :—" A proclamation was addressed to the inhabitants of the towns and provinces in the south of France, and assurances given that the coalesced powers (the English, the Spaniards, the Neapolitans, and Sardinians) would willingly co-operate with the well-disposed in putting down the odious faction that governed the country.

" The town of Toulon," he writes, " which occupies the north side of the harbour, is fortified with great art, both on the land and sea approaches, but, being commanded by the heights with which it is surrounded on all sides, must be dependent on them for protection. A semicircular chain of mountains on the north extends from the Hières road on the east to the pass of Oliol on the west ; this pass, which is five miles from the town, might have bid defiance to any force had it been guarded by British troops."

" Before Lord Hood with his fleet entered the road of Toulon," writes Captain Brenton, " it was judged necessary that the forts commanding that anchorage should be put into possession of British officers and men, which was accordingly effected at midnight on the 27th, when 1700 marines and seamen from the different ships were landed, under the command of Captain the Honourable George Keith Elphinstone, of the *Robust*, who received an appointment from the admiral as governor of Fort La Malgue, commanding, by its situation, both the town and the inner and outer roads. The British and Spanish fleets entered the great road at the same time, the Spanish division under the command of Admiral Gravina. The British fleet anchored in the bay, and Rear-Admiral Goodall was appointed governor of Toulon."

According to Mr. James, Lord Hood's force when he entered the bay of Toulon consisted of twenty-one sail of the line, besides frigates and sloops. He gives a list of the larger vessels, with the names of their commanders, and among them appears the *Windsor Castle*, ninety-eight guns, Vice-Admiral Cosby's flag-ship, commanded by Captain Sir Thomas Byard, and the *Agamemnon*, commanded by England's greatest naval hero, Horatio Nelson, who at that time had only attained the rank of captain.

No sooner had the English and their allies taken possession of the forts on the heights surrounding Toulon, and those at the entrance of the harbour, than the Republicans, having, as Captain Brenton remarks, " resolved at once to regain possession of

the place, and to gratify their revenge by the destruction of the Royalists, lost no time in con-
centrating their forces round this devoted town.
The armies of the Republic approached it from
the east, west, and north." And he adds:—"It was
on this occasion that the celebrated Napoleon
Bonaparte first made himself conspicuous; his
talents and courage were greatly instrumental in
the reduction of Toulon. A lieutenant-colonel of
artillery, he had the art and the audacity to command respect and obedience even from his superior
officers, who blindly submitted to be led by him.
And to him the Convention owed the surrender
of the place and the retreat of the British and their
allies."

"During the time that Toulon remained in the
possession of the allied forces," Mr. James writes, "a
very formidable insurrection" [against the French]
"existed in Corsica, and General Paoli, the leader
of the insurgent party, sought the aid of the English, assuring Lord Hood that even the appearance
of a few ships off the island would be of the most
essential service to the popular cause. Accordingly,
in the month of September, a squadron, composed
of the following line-of-battle ships and frigates,
sailed from Toulon for Villa-Franca:—*Alcide* (74
guns), Commodore Robert Linzee, Captain John
Woodley; *Courageux* (74 guns), Captain John
Matthews; *Ardent* (64 guns), Captain Robert
Manners Sutton. Frigates—*Lowestoffe* (32 guns),

Captain William Wolseley; *Nemesis* (28 guns), Captain Lord Emilius Beauclerk.

"On his arrival off Villa-Franca, Commodore Linzee, in conformity to the orders he had received, sent a letter on shore containing the account of the restoration of monarchy at Toulon, as well as copies of the proclamation that had been addressed by Lord Hood to the inhabitants of the south of France. To this communication no answer was returned. The commodore then stood across to the island of Corsica, and showed his force off Calvi and San Fiorenzo, meeting from the respective inhabitants no better reception than he had experienced at Villa-Franca, except that a few of the mountaineers came down, and were supplied, at their own request, with muskets and ammunition. His offers did not persuade, nor his force intimidate, the garrisons, although accompanied by an assurance that the latter, if desirous, should be conveyed to France.

"The orders of the British commodore, in the event of a refusal on the part of the garrisons, were to attempt their reduction by force; or, should that appear too hazardous, to invest the places with his ships, and starve the inhabitants into a compliance. To blockade three such ports as Calvi, San Fiorenzo, and Bastia with three line-of-battle ships and two frigates was impracticable; but Commodore Linzee, having been led to believe that the batteries of San Fiorenzo could not, on account of the distance, co-operate with the tower and redoubt of Fornelli, situated about two miles in advance of the town, thought he might make an advantageous attack by sea on that formidable post.

" It being necessary, previous to an attack upon Fornelli, to get possession of a tower that commanded the only secure anchorage in the Gulf of San Fiorenzo, the *Lowestoffe* and *Nemesis* frigates were detached upon that service. As soon as" [Captain Wolseley's vessel] "the *Lowestoffe*, which, in working up to Cape Martello, had got to windward of her consort, arrived within gunshot of the tower, she opened a fire upon it; then stood out, and on tacking in again, repeated the fire.[1] Just as the third broadside was about to be bestowed, a boat was seen to quit the shore and pull in the direction of the town of San Fiorenzo. Captain Wolseley immediately despatched two boats, with Lieutenants John Gibbs and Francis Charles Annesley, and thirty men, to take possession of the tower.

" The British landed without opposition, and although the ladder leading to the entrance, which was by an opening about twenty feet up the wall of the building, had been carried off by the fugitives, the seamen, by means of some spars found on the spot, managed to gain admission. Three long guns, one 24 and two 18-pounders, were found mounted

---

[1] Probably these tactics were for the purpose of getting out of range, and avoiding the return shots from the tower.

on the top of this extraordinary tower (named
Martello, after its inventor, Monsieur Martel); but
before the garrison fled the powder had all been
thrown into the well. On observing the *Lowestoffe's*
success, the *Nemesis* bore away to the commodore
with the intelligence, and the squadron soon afterwards entered the bay and came to an anchor."

After possession had been taken of the tower,
Captain Wolseley went to inspect it, and was so
struck by the peculiar construction of the little
fortress that he took a plan of it, which was forwarded to the British Government; and soon after,
the "Martello" towers on our own coasts were
constructed. They do not appear, however, to have
had much resemblance to the one from which they
were supposed to have been copied, and which is
thus described by Captain Brenton:—"This tower,"
he writes, "was of an extraordinary and ingenious
construction, about fifty feet in diameter, by forty-
five high, and of a circular form; the walls were
twelve feet thick; the parapet was lined with bass-
junk,[1] a kind of cable made of grass, and the
interstices were filled up with wet sand." He then
gives an account of the armament, and differs from
Mr. James as to the number of guns; but as the
latter took his information from the official *Gazette*,
and also mentions the way in which Admiral Linzee
afterwards disposed of the three guns found in the

---

[1] Mr. James states that it was lined with bass-junk "to the depth of
five feet."

tower, his statement is likely to have been more correct than that of Captain Brenton, who merely says that there was only one gun, from his own recollection of a model he saw of the tower, "with the exact account of its furniture and equipment." He mentions that "there was a well of water" in the fortress; and Mr. James says that there was also in it "a furnace for heating shot."

On the 1st of October an unsuccessful attack was made on Fornelli by Commodore Linzee with the ships *Ardent*, *Alcide*, and *Courageux*, but being exposed to a raking fire both from the redoubt and also from the town of San Fiorenzo, and as the vessels were greatly damaged, and there were also great losses among the crews, both in killed and wounded, he had to discontinue the attack and retire. The two frigates, the *Lowestoffe* and the *Nemesis*, do not seem to have been engaged, as they are not mentioned by Mr. James, and probably they had previously been sent off on some other service. Before he left the bay Commodore Linzee gave up the tower of Martello to the Corsicans under General Paoli. But on the 24th of the month it was recaptured by the French under Commodore Perée, who was in command of a squadron consisting of four frigates and a brig-corvette.

Mr. James says:—"While the British fleet lay at Toulon, Lord Hood occasionally sent small detachments in quest of the remaining ships of the Toulon fleet, still, according to information received, cruising in the Mediterranean seas." And he states that on the 22nd October, Captain Horatio Nelson, while cruising in his ship, the *Agamemnon*, off the coast of Sardinia, saw this squadron, and attacked and chased, "with every stitch of canvas set," one of the frigates, but it succeeded in joining the other vessels and in getting away. The *Agamemnon*, "having her main-topsail cut to pieces, main and mizzen masts and foreyard badly injured, and a great quantity of rigging shot away," could not follow; and "on the 24th," he continues, "the *Agamemnon* anchored in Cagliari Bay to repair her damages, and the French frigates proceeded to Martello Bay. From this anchorage," he adds, "they might probably have been compelled to remove by the fire of the tower, which, as elsewhere stated, had been captured in the preceding month by the *Lowestoffe*, but Commodore Linzee had since removed the guns into a tender which he chose to fit out. The consequence was, that the Corsicans left in charge had no alternative but to abandon the tower, and a party from the French squadron immediately landed and took possession of it."

In the meantime the position of the English and their allies at Toulon had become very precarious. During the time they occupied Toulon they were constantly harassed by attacks of overwhelming forces of the Republicans; and in the middle of December, when their position became untenable, Captain Brenton says, "Lieutenant-General Dundas addressed a letter to the Secretary of War, in which, after detailing the noble exertions of his troops, and the events which had brought himself and his companions to that mortifying situation, he gave such an account of the strength and resources of the enemy, compared with his own, as leaves us astonished at the magnanimity which could persevere under such insurmountable difficulties. 'From concurring testimonies (says the General), the enemy's army now amounted to between thirty and forty thousand men'; and 'for the complete defence of the town and harbour, we have been long obliged to occupy a circumference of at least fifteen miles by eight, principal posts, with their several intermediate ones. The greatest part of these were of a temporary nature, such as our means allowed us to construct; and of our force, which never exceeded 12,000 men bearing arms, composed of five different nations and languages, nearly 9000 were placed in or supporting these posts, and about 3000 remained in the town.'"

"On the night of the 14th" (December 1793), writes Mr. James, "in the midst of a storm, the French marched from their encampments in three columns, each column taking a route leading to a different point of the line of posts, so that their attacks might be simultaneous"; and during the next few days the besiegers continued to bombard the works with considerable effect.

Napoleon Buonaparte himself was present in these

attacks ; and a French author, quoted by Mr. James, says of him, "Un jeune homme de vingt-trois ans fut jugé capable et digne du commande-ment de l'artillerie ; on la lui confia." And he then tells the following anecdote :—"À l'attaque de fort Pharon, un commissaire de la convention critique et condamne la position d'une batterie. Buonaparte lui dit avec fierté, 'Melez-vous de votre métier de réprésentant ; laissez-moi faire le mien d'artilleur ; cette batterie restera là, et je réponds du succès.'" "The battery," writes Mr. James, "did fully succeed, and Buonaparte received the applause of the generals present, and shortly afterwards was himself made a brigadier-general."

On the 17th the French succeeded in forcing all the posts on the mountains of Pharon, and "thus," writes Mr. James, "was the line of defence broken in upon its two most essential points, and the ships in the harbour and the town itself were overawed by the very cannon which had been mounted for their protection. Most of the ships, indeed, were compelled to unmoor and retire to a safer position.

"Things being thus situated, a council of war was immediately held," and "it was unanimously resolved that Toulon should be evacuated as soon as proper arrangements could be made for that purpose." It was also decided that the French ships of war "which were armed[1] should sail out

[1] These armed ships had Royalist officers and crews. The crews of the others were Republicans.

with the fleet, and that those which remained in the harbour, together with the magazines and the arsenal, should be destroyed."

Mr. James and Captain Brenton give most interesting and graphic accounts of the events that occurred on the afternoon of the 18th, when, as the first-mentioned author says, "the important service of destroying the ships and magazines was entrusted, at his own particular request, to Captain Sir Sidney Smith" (afterwards Admiral Sir Sidney Smith). The commencement of the conflagration of the shipping had been the signal for evacuating the town ; and the whole of the troops embarked, and were on board the fleet by daylight on the morning of the 19th, " without," writes Mr. James, "the loss of a man," although the vessels were repeatedly fired at as they were leaving the harbour ; and in his description of the fortifications of Toulon, previously given, he states that "at the mouth of the basin are two jetties, and the outer sides of these present two tremendous batteries, à fleur d'eau, or nearly even with the water's edge—the very worst species of fort for a ship to encounter."

Captain Brenton mentions that the English took away with them three French ships of the line, the *Commerce de Marseilles*, of one hundred and twenty guns ; the *Pompée*, of eighty ; and *Puissant*, of seventy-four ; and says that "on the first alarm" these ships "were quickly filled with [Royalist] emigrants of all ranks, ages, and sexes, flying from inevitable destruction"; and he adds that "the officers and crews of the British ships of war rendered every assistance in their power to these unhappy fugitives," and that "the *Princess Royal* had on board, at one time, nearly four thousand people, and the *Robust* three thousand, besides their own crews." These people were afterwards distributed into the different ships of the fleet; and as soon as circumstances would admit of that arrangement, they were landed in Corsica, Italy, and elsewhere, and many of them, doubtless, took refuge in England.

CHAPTER IV

As Captain Brenton justly remarks, Lord Hood, in engaging "to defend the inhabitants of Toulon and Marseilles against the immense armies of the Republic, without having the means of doing so, or knowing the number and strength of the forces he had to encounter, had certainly taken upon himself a greater degree of responsibility than he was aware of.

"After the night of the 18th of December he retreated with his fleet to Hières Bay, a fine anchorage about ten miles east of Toulon." He was accompanied by the French admiral, Trogoffe, and his three ships of the line bearing the white flag. These vessels, the *Commerce de Marseilles*, the *Pompée*, and the *Puissant*, previously mentioned, are stated by Captain Brenton to have been taken into the British service in the course of the following year, but he says that "all their officers and crews were previously discharged."

"Driven from the Continent," he writes, "the two commanders-in-chief," Lord Hood and General Dundas, "next considered where the forces under their orders might be the most beneficially employed for the advantage of the public service, when the island of Corsica, a colony of France, and not more than eighty miles from the anchorage they now occupied, appeared to them to afford the fairest prospect of success. This romantic spot had, in the year 1789, at the request of the Corsicans, through General Paoli, been declared the eighty-third department of France; but in consequence of the events of the Revolution, which was felt to the utmost parts of the world where the French had any influence, the Corsicans became restless, revolted again from their new masters, and Paoli, at their instigation, sent an invitation to Lord Hood to come and take possession of the island."

Dr. Southey, in his "Life of Nelson," gives a short sketch of the previous history of Corsica, and also of that of General Paoli; and before entering on the account of the warfare in Corsica, I give a few extracts that may, perhaps, interest the reader.

"About thirty years before this time," writes Dr. Southey, "the heroic patriotism of the Corsicans, and of their leader Paoli (father of the general), had been the admiration of England. The history of these brave people," he continues, "is but a melancholy tale. The Moors, the Pisans, the kings of Aragon, and the Genoese successively attempted, and each for a time effected, its conquest. The yoke of the Genoese continued longest, and was the heaviest. These petty tyrants ruled with an iron rod; and when at any time a patriot rose to resist their oppressions, if they failed to subdue him by force, they resorted to assassination."

In the early part of the eighteenth century, the Corsicans having risen against their oppressors, Genoa called in the French to her assistance, which, as Dr. Southey remarks, was readily given. "For such was their ascendency at Genoa," he writes, "that in subduing Corsica for these allies, they were, in fact, subduing it for themselves. They entered into the contest, therefore, with their usual vigour and their usual cruelty. It was in vain that the Corsicans addressed a most affecting memorial to the Court of Versailles ; that remorseless Government persisted in its flagitious project. They poured in troops, dressed a part of them like the people of the country, by which means they deceived and destroyed many of the patriots ; cut down the standing corn, the vines, and the olives ; set fire to the villages, and hung all the most able and active men who fell into their hands. A war of this kind may be carried on with success against a country so small and so thinly peopled as Corsica. Having reduced the island to perfect servitude, which they called peace, the French withdrew their forces."

"General Paoli's father was one of the patriots who effected their escape from Corsica when the French reduced it to obedience. He retired to Naples, and brought up this his youngest son in the Neapolitan service." Some years later, after a desultory warfare which had continued for two years, "the Corsicans," writes Dr. Southey, "heard of young Paoli's abilities, and solicited him to come over to his native country and take the command." When Paoli arrived "he formed a democratical government, of which he was chosen chief; he restored the authority of the laws, estab-lished an university, and took such measures, both for repressing abuses and moulding the rising gene-ration, that, if France had not interfered, Corsica might at this day have been as free and flourish-ing and happy a commonwealth as any of the Grecian states in the days of their prosperity. The Genoese were at this time driven out of their for-tified towns, and must in a short time have been expelled. France was indebted some millions of livres to Genoa; it was not convenient to pay this money; so the French Minister proposed to the Genoese that she should discharge the debt by sending six battalions to serve in Corsica for four years.

"The immediate object of the French," continues Dr. Southey, "happened to be purely mercenary; they wanted to clear off their debt to Genoa; and as the presence of their troops in the island effected this, they aimed at doing the people no further mischief. . . . But when the four years were ex-pired, France purchased the sovereignty of Corsica from the Genoese for forty millions of livres.

"A desperate and glorious resistance was made

by the Corsicans, but it was in vain"; and, Dr.
Southey continues, "no power interposed in behalf
of these injured islanders, and the French poured
in as many troops as were required. They offered
to confirm Paoli in the supreme authority, on condition that he would hold it under their government."
He declined the offer with contempt, and "they
then set a price upon his head. During two campaigns he kept them at bay; but they overpowered
him at length. He was driven to the shore, and
having escaped on ship-board, took refuge in
England," where "he was welcomed," Dr. Southey
says, "with the honours which he deserved; a
pension of £1200 per annum was immediately
granted him, and provision was liberally made for
his elder brother and his nephew.

"Above twenty years," continues Dr. Southey,
"Paoli remained in England. But when the French
Revolution began, it seemed as if the restoration of
Corsica was at hand. The whole country, as if
animated by one spirit, rose and demanded liberty;
and the National Assembly passed a decree recog-
nising the island as a department of France, and
therefore entitled to all the privileges of the new
French constitution. This satisfied the Corsicans,
and Paoli, in whom the ardour of youth was past,
seeing that his countrymen were contented, and
believing that they were about to enjoy a state of
freedom, naturally wished to return to his native
land. He resigned his pension in the year 1790,

and appeared at the bar of the Assembly with the Corsican deputies when they took the oath of fidelity to France. But the course of events in France soon dispelled those hopes of a new and better order of things which Paoli, in common with so many friends of humankind, had indulged; and perceiving, after the execution of the King, that a civil war was about to ensue, of which no man could foresee the issue, he prepared to break the connection between Corsica and the French Republic. The Convention, suspecting such a design, and perhaps occasioning it by their suspicions, ordered him to their bar. That way, he well knew, led to the guillotine, and returning a respectful answer, he pleaded age and infirmity as a reason for disobeying the summons.

" He then repaired to Corté, the capital of the island, and was again invested with the authority which he had held in the noonday of his fame. The Convention, upon this, denounced him as a rebel and set a price upon his head." Paoli now opened the correspondence with Lord Hood which led to Commodore Linzee's being sent to assist him. But, as already related, Paoli was not ready at the time to assist in an attack upon St. Fiorenzo, and Commodore Linzee's attempt was not successful.

" After the evacuation of Toulon, Lord Hood," writes Dr. Southey, "despatched Lieutenant-Colonel (afterwards Sir John) Moore and Major Koehler to confer with Paoli upon a plan of operations. Sir Gilbert Elliot accompanied them; and it was agreed upon, that in consideration of the succours, both military and naval, which his Britannic Majesty should afford for the purpose of expelling the French, the island of Corsica should be delivered into the immediate possession of his Majesty, and bind itself to acquiesce in any settlement he might approve of concerning its government and its future relations with Great Britain."

A few months later "the sovereignty of the island was vested in the King of England, to whom," writes Captain Brenton, "the people swore allegiance; and Sir Gilbert Elliot, afterwards Lord Minto, was appointed Viceroy, the British constitution proclaimed, and its laws declared to be those of the new conquest. The deputies having met at Corté in sufficient numbers to constitute a National Assembly," he continues, "chose General Paoli as their President, and formally declared, first, their separation from France, and, secondly, their union to the crown of Great Britain."

After this somewhat long digression, however, I now return to my narrative of the events which led to this result. As the reader will remember, an account has already been given in the last chapter of a previous expedition to Corsica in which Captain Wolseley, in his vessel the *Lowestoffe*, served under the command of Commodore Linzee, who had been sent by Lord Hood for the purpose of making an attack upon St. Fiorenzo by sea;

General Paoli having engaged to attack it by land at the same time. This promise the general was unable to perform, and, in consequence, Commodore Linzee, who, in reliance upon it, was sent upon this service, was repulsed with some loss. But after the evacuation of Toulon, with a larger force at their disposal, Lord Hood and General Dundas decided upon going to the assistance of the loyal part of the inhabitants of Corsica in an attempt to expel the French from the island.

"Accordingly," writes Mr. James, "on the 24th of January,[1] at 4 P.M., the British fleet, amounting, including transports, to sixty sail, got under way from the Bay of Hières, and proceeded towards the Bay of St. Fiorenzo. On the next day, the 25th, a gale of wind came on, and dispersed and endangered the fleet; the *Victory*, Lord Hood's flag-ship, among other ships, having two main-top-sails blown to rags, and the yard itself rendered totally unserviceable. On the 29th the fleet, being driven greatly to leeward, gained, but not without difficulty, Porto Ferrajo, in the island of Elba. As three-decked ships were not qualified to navigate narrow seas and rocky coasts, particularly in the winter season, the 74-gun ships, the *Alcide* (Captain John Woodley), bearing the flag of Commodore Linzee, the *Egmont* (Captain Archibald Dickson),

---

[1] Captain Brenton says "February"; but this is evidently a mistake as the dates mentioned by Mr. James coincide with those given by Admiral Wolseley.

and *Fortitude* (Captain William Young), accompanied by two frigates, the *Lowestoffe*" [Captain
William Wolseley] "and the *Juno*, and by several
transports with troops, were detached on the 5th
of February to a bay lying to the westward of
Martello, where they arrived in safety on the 7th.
On the same evening the troops, in number about
1400, commanded by Major-General Dundas, disembarked, and immediately took possession of a
height which overlooked the tower of Martello,
the first of several strong positions necessary to be
reduced before the anchorage at the west side of
the Gulf of St. Fiorenzo could be made properly
secure, and which tower, it will be recollected, had
been recaptured from the Corsicans, in the October
of the preceding year, by a squadron of French
frigates."

"The tower," writes Mr. James, "mounted one
6 and two 18-pounders. These guns had been
brought on shore from the French frigates, when
they retook it in October." The garrison, thirty-
three men in number, "maintained their post until
it was no longer tenable"; and Admiral Wolseley
says, in the memoir previously quoted:—"On the
9th of February," when the attack was made, "this
tower beat off, after two hours and a half cannon-
ading, the *Fortitude*, seventy-four guns (this ship
was twice set on fire), and the *Juno*, thirty-two
guns; more than sixty men being killed and
wounded in the two ships." "The battering from

F

the height on shore," Mr. James continues, "had
been as unsuccessful as that from the ships, till
some additional pieces were mounted and hot shot
used, when one of the latter, falling among and
setting fire to the bass-junk with which, to the
depth of five feet, the immensely thick parapet was
lined, induced the garrison to call for quarter." [1]

"The next post to be attacked," writes Mr.
James (and in this service Captain Wolseley was
employed), "was the Convention redoubt, mounted
with twenty-one pieces of heavy ordnance, and
considered as the key of St. Fiorenzo. By the
most surprising exertions of science and labour on
the part of the officers and men of the navy, several
18-pounders and other pieces were placed on an
eminence of very difficult ascent, 700 feet above
the level of the sea. This rocky elevation, owing
to its perpendicularity near its summit, was deemed
inaccessible; but the seamen, by means of blocks
and ropes, contrived to haul up the guns, each of
which weighed about forty - two hundredweight.
The path along which these dauntless fellows crept
would, in most places, admit but one person at a
time. On the right was a descent of many hundred
feet, and one false step would have led to eternity;
on the left were stupendous overhanging rocks,

---

[1] On the evacuation of the island in the following year, the tower
was blown up. Lord St. Vincent says in a letter to the Viceroy of
Corsica (dated " *Victory*, in Martello Bay, 27th October 1796 ") :—
"The Martello Tower was effectually demolished at eight o'clock
last night."

which occasionally served as fixed points for the tackle employed in raising the guns. From these 18-pounders, so admirably posted, a cannonade was unremittingly kept up during the whole of the 16th and 17th. On the latter evening, when the fire of the redoubt had become nearly overpowered, it was determined to storm the works, a service which was executed with vigour and crowned with success.

"A part only of the garrison were made prisoners ; the remainder retired to another stronghold which was distant about 400 yards, and separated by a deep ravine from the former. That post the Republicans abandoned about midnight ; then crossed over to the town of St. Fiorenzo, with their two frigates, and left the British in quiet possession of the tower and batteries of Fornelli."

In the account of the storming of Fornelli given by Captain Brenton, that officer says : — "The mountains which overlooked this post were deemed by many to be inaccessible, and probably few but Englishmen would have attempted to place guns in such a situation." And he adds :—"In all conjoint expeditions of the army and navy, the landing or transporting of cannon is performed by the seamen, after which the artillery officers mount the guns and complete the batteries. This work was executed in such a manner as to call forth the highest eulogiums from General Dundas, the commander-in-chief of the land forces. "In four days," says the general, "by the most surprising exertions of science and labour, they had placed four 18-pounders, a large howitzer, and a 10-inch mortar, in battery, on a ground elevated 700 feet above the level of the sea, and where every difficulty of ascent and surface opposed their undertaking."

It was mentioned in despatches that when "the heights of Fornelli were carried, Captain Wolseley had particularly distinguished himself"; and very shortly afterwards he was commissioned to the *Impérieuse*, a prize frigate—a much larger and finer ship than the *Lowestoffe*.

On the 18th, after the works of Fornelli had been abandoned by the enemy, the squadron anchored in Martello Bay. The next day, the 19th, two French frigates were taken; and "on the same evening," writes Mr. James, "St. Fiorenzo, with its formidable batteries, mounting 25 pieces of cannon, including two 12-inch mortars, two 36 and seven 24-pounders, were taken possession of by the British."

The French having retreated to Bastia, Lord Hood submitted to General Dundas, who commanded the land forces, a plan for the reduction of that place. But, as Mr. James writes, "having failed to convince Major-General Dundas of the practicability of reducing Bastia with the small forces which had already effected so much, Lord Hood sailed from St. Fiorenzo Bay on the evening of the 23rd, to try what effect the appearance of his fleet alone would produce. After cruising off the port for a fortnight, and gaining every intelligence necessary to facilitate his plans, the British admiral, with a part of his squadron, sailed back to St. Fiorenzo Bay, where he arrived on the 5th of March. The major-general still declining to act until the arrival of an expected reinforcement of two thousand men from Gibraltar, Lord Hood took on board that proportion of the land forces which had originally been ordered to serve on board the fleet as marines, and obtained, also, two officers and thirty privates of artillery, with ordnance-stores and intrenching tools.

"With this force, on the 2nd of April, Lord Hood again set sail for, and on the 4th arrived at, the anchorage before Bastia. On the same evening the troops, commanded by Lieutenant-Colonel Vilettes, with the guns, mortars, and ordnance-stores, and also a detachment of seamen commanded by Captain Horatio Nelson of the *Agamemnon*, were under the able superintendence of the latter, disembarked at a spot a little to the northward of the town. The total of the combined forces, when landed, amounted to 1248 officers and men, exclusive of the Corsicans, under General Paoli, in number about the same; and the number of French and Corsican troops in garrison at Bastia was, as it afterwards appeared, 3000."

"Guns," writes Dr. Southey in his "Life of Nelson," "were dragged by the sailors up heights where it appeared almost impossible to convey

them—a work of the greatest difficulty, and which
Nelson said could never, in his opinion, have been
accomplished by any but British seamen. The
soldiers, though less dexterous in such service,
because not accustomed, like sailors, to habitual
dexterity, behaved with equal spirit. ' Their zeal,'
said Nelson, who had now acquired from them the
title of Brigadier, 'is almost unexampled. There is
not a man but considers himself as personally inter-
ested in the event, and deserted by the general. It
has, I am persuaded, made them equal to double
their numbers.'"

Before the siege began, General Dundas sent a
reconnoitring party from St. Fiorenzo to the heights
above Bastia ; and although he had five regiments
at St. Fiorenzo, he said in a letter to Lord Hood :
—" After mature consideration, and a personal in-
spection for several days of all circumstances, local
as well as others, I consider the siege of Bastia,
with our present means and force, to be a most
visionary and rash attempt, such as no officer would
be justified in undertaking." " Lord Hood," continues Dr. Southey, "replied that nothing would be
more gratifying to his feelings than to have the
whole responsibility upon himself, and that he was
ready and willing to undertake the reduction of the
place at his own risk, with the force and means
already there. General d'Aubant, who succeeded
at this time to the command of the army, coincided
in opinion with his predecessor, and did not think

it right to furnish his lordship with a single soldier,
cannon, or any stores." In the meantime, as Dr.
Southey says, "the French had improved the
leisure which our military commander had allowed
them, and before Lord Hood commenced his
operations, he had the mortification of seeing that
the enemy were every day erecting new works,
strengthening old ones, and rendering the attempt
more difficult."

"On the 11th," writes Mr. James, "the British
batteries, which had been erected on several commanding heights, being ready to be opened, Lord
Hood sent a written summons to the town, but
which the French general, Lacombe St. Michael,
would not even read." And, as related by Dr.
Southey, he replied in these terms to the English
general:—"I have hot shot for your ships, and
bayonets for your troops. When two-thirds of our
men are killed, I will then trust to the generosity
of the English." Mr. James continues:—"At the
appointed signal, therefore, the batteries, consisting
of five 24-pounders, two 13 and two 10-inch mortars, and two heavy carronades, commenced their
fire upon the enemy's works, and were promptly
answered by the numerous guns with which the
latter were crowned.

"At length, on the 21st of May, after a siege
of thirty-seven and a negotiation of four days, the
town and citadel of Bastia, with the several posts
upon the neighbouring heights, surrendered;" and

immediately afterwards, according to Dr. Southey, "on the following morning, General d'Aubant arrived with the whole army to take possession of Bastia."

"The event of this siege," continues the same writer, "had justified the confidence of the sailors; but they themselves excused the opinion of the generals when they saw what they had done. "I am all astonishment," said Nelson, "when I reflect upon what we have achieved; 1000 regulars, 1500 National Guards, and a large party of Corsican troops, 4000 in all, laying down their arms to 1200 soldiers, marines, and seamen! I always was of opinion, have ever acted up to it, and never had any reason to repent it, that one Englishman was equal to three Frenchmen. Had this been an English town, I am sure it would not have been taken by them."

The reader will probably observe that there is a slight discrepancy between the numbers of the besiegers and besieged given by Mr. James and by Lord Nelson. It is, however, certain that the English were not nearly equal in strength to the French, though, as Dr. Southey remarks, "when it had been resolved to attack the place, the enemy were supposed to be far inferior in number" to what was afterwards ascertained; "and," he adds, "it was not till the whole had been arranged and the siege publicly undertaken that Nelson received certain information of the great superiority of the garrison. This intelligence he kept secret, fearing lest, if so fair a pretext were afforded, the attempt would be abandoned."

Admiral Wolseley's presence at the siege of Bastia, in which the British navy so greatly distinguished itself, is mentioned by Lord Nelson, and also by General Paoli, in letters written to him by these two celebrated men at a somewhat later date. But apparently he was not present when the garrison of Bastia capitulated, as Mr. James says:—"The enemy had magazines of provisions and stores on the island of Capraja, and the recently captured frigate, *Impérieuse*, Captain William Wolseley, was despatched thither, and effectually prevented the Republicans from making use of them."

"One of the cartel's ships, which afterwards carried the garrison of Bastia to Toulon," writes Dr. Southey, "brought back intelligence that the French were about to sail from that port—such exertions had they made to repair the damage done at the evacuation, and to fit out a fleet."

According to Mr. James, the French fleet, consisting of seven sail of the line and four or five frigates, put out to sea on the 5th of June. "Lord Hood, who, as already stated, then lay off Bastia, departed, the moment he received the information, with thirteen sail of the line and four frigates." Mr. James then gives a list of the ships and the names of their commanders. Included in this

list appears the "*Windsor Castle*, Vice-Admiral Philipps Cosby, Captain Sir Thomas Byard"; but, curiously enough, he omits the name of the *Agamemnon*, commanded by Nelson, who was certainly with them at that time, as Dr. Southey says, "Lord Hood sailed in quest of the French fleet, towards the islands of the Hières. The *Agamemnon* was with him"; and then gives an extract from a letter written by Nelson to his wife on that occasion, expressing his hopes that they might meet the French fleet.

Captain Wolseley's vessel, the *Impérieuse*, is not named in the list either, and he himself gives no details about his services at that period. But after the fall of Bastia, as there could have been no further occasion for keeping a watch on the island of Capraja, he probably went on this expedition with the rest of the fleet. It, however, had no result, as the French fleet escaped; and Mr. James continues :—"On the 10th the two fleets gained sight of each other; the British immediately made all sail in chase. On the 11th, at daylight, the British and French admirals were between three and four leagues apart. To avoid an action with a force so superior, M. Martin pushed for the anchorage in Gourjean Bay, which he reached with his fleet about 2 P.M. But none of the British ships were able to get near, except the 28-gun frigate, *Dido*, Captain Towry, who received and gallantly returned the fire of some of the rear ships, as well as of two forts that guarded the entrance of the anchorage."

"The wind fell," writes Dr. Southey, "and prevented Lord Hood from getting between them and the shore, as he designed. Boats came out from Antibes and other places to their assistance, and towed them within the shoals in Gourjean roads, where they were protected by batteries on isles St. Honoré and St. Marguerite, and on Cape Garousse."

The change of wind having prevented Lord Hood from attacking them, he left Admiral Hotham with a squadron to watch them, and proceeded to assist in the reduction of Calvi, which was still in the possession of a Republican garrison. The *Impérieuse*, Captain Wolseley's ship, was one of those employed in the siege ; and the *Agamemnon* was at once "despatched," writes Dr. Southey, "to co-operate with General Sir Charles Stuart," who had arrived with the expected reinforcement of troops from Gibraltar. Nelson's ship, according to the account given by Mr. James, "carried the troops to Port Agra, a small cove about three miles from Calvi." And he continues : —"On the 19th of June the whole of the men disembarked, and on the same evening encamped in a strong position upon a neighbouring ridge. Lord Hood, returning on that day to Martello Bay, sent a detachment of the *Victory's* seamen, with some ordnance and other stores, under the orders of Captains Hallowell and Serocold, to Calvi. On the 27th he arrived himself before that place in the *Victory*, and immediately landed seven of his first deck guns, for the use of the batteries constructed to act against the town and its powerful defences."

"The siege of Calvi," writes Captain Brenton, "was pressed with the greatest vigour, both by land and sea." He adds :—"Calvi lies in a deep bay on the north-west side of the island; it held out for fifty-one days, and capitulated after a close siege and a rigorous blockade by sea. The fort of Mollinochesco," he continues, "situated on a steep rock, commanded the communication between Calvi and the province of Ballagni, from which it was considerably in advance. The bomb-proof fort of Mozello, well mounted with heavy artillery, guarded the approaches to Calvi, which was of itself both by nature and art a strongly fortified town. Two frigates lay in the bay, and supported by their fire the works of the enemy. These important outposts were speedily reduced by batteries formed on the heights, which, like those of Fiorenzo, had hitherto been deemed inaccessible. The frigates and all the vessels in the bay were compelled to take refuge under the guns of the town. Lieutenant-Colonel (afterwards the gallant and ill-fated Sir John) Moore, of the 51st Regiment, with Major Brereton, of the 30th, proceeded with the cool determination of British soldiers through a heavy fire into the breach of Mollinochesco with fixed bayonets and unloaded arms. They quickly dislodged the enemy from their stronghold, carrying the trenches on the left with equal intrepidity. Possessed of all his important outposts, and with batteries advanced within six hundred yards of the walls of the town, General Stuart offered the commandant terms of capitulation, which were haughtily rejected, and the siege was renewed for nine days more, when a severe bombardment of eighteen hours induced them to surrender."

" But not," writes Mr. James, "till the siege had lasted fifty-one days could General Casa Bianca be induced to capitulate. This he did on the 10th of August, upon terms highly flattering to the bravery of the garrison of Calvi. The loss sustained by the enemy," James adds, "does not appear in the published accounts." But that "on the part of the British army amounted to one field-officer, two lieutenants, and twenty privates killed, and three captains, four lieutenants, and forty-six non-commissioned officers and privates wounded ; and on the part of the British navy, to one captain (Walter Serocold, by a grape-shot at the principal battery while getting the last gun into its place), one midshipman, and five seamen killed, and six seamen wounded. Among the non-reported wounded was Captain Nelson, who lost his eye in consequence of a shot striking the battery near him, and driving some particles of sand with considerable force into it.

"Among the vessels found in the port of Calvi, and delivered up to the British, were the French frigates *Melpomène* and *Mignonne*. The latter mounted thirty-two guns, and was small and of little value. The *Melpomène*, on the contrary, was a fine 40-gun frigate of 1014 tons, and was added to the British navy as a cruising frigate. A considerable quantity of naval stores also fell into the hands of the British."

Dr. Southey mentions that "Nelson had less responsibility at Calvi than at Bastia, and was acting with a general after his own heart, who was never sparing of himself, and slept every night in the advanced battery. But the service was not less hard," he adds, "than that of the former siege"; and he remarks a little farther on that "the climate proved more destructive than the service, for this was during the period of the 'lion sun,' as they there call our season of the 'dog days.' Of 2000 men above half were sick, and the rest like so many phantoms." But he adds, "Nelson said to Lord Hood, 'We will fag ourselves to death before any blame shall lie at our doors. And I trust it will not be forgotten that twenty-five pieces of heavy ordnance have been dragged to the different batteries, mounted, and all but three fought by seamen, except one artilleryman to point the guns."

"By the fall of Calvi," as Captain Brenton remarks, "the last remains of the French were expelled from Corsica." After the siege was ended, Admiral

Wolseley had the honour of being again mentioned in despatches by Lord Hood, who, on this occasion, spoke highly of "the meritorious conduct" and "steady perseverance" of Captain Wolseley, whose services during the warfare in Corsica were also mentioned in the most complimentary manner in a letter written to him by the celebrated Corsican general, Pasquale Paoli. Captain Wolseley had, apparently, given a friend a letter of introduction to the general, who in reply wrote the following letter :—

" OVERRACHE, *1st of September* 1794.

" MY DEAR SIR,—I have to-day the honour of your letter of the 16 august, sent me by Mr. Tudory.[1] The liberty which my countrimen now enjoy out of any apprehension of being deprived of it again by the French, shall be an everlasting motive of gratitude and attachement to the generous English Nation and King, who has taken them under his protection, and sent to their assistance souch a powerfull fleet and brave army. And I am acquainted too that many obligations we owe to your activity and zeal shown in the sieges of St. Floreint, Bastia, and Calvi ; and pray, you will receive my best acknolegement of them in the name too of my countrimen.

" I have wrote in favour Mr. Tudory upon your recommendation ; at my campe some gentlemen

---

[1] The name was, probably, Tudor ;—but I have left it as written by General Paoli.

tooke a share in the armament, and are souch, that
I am sure they wont permit any wrong to pass
against his interest.

"I hope Sir to have some other occasion to show
you the true esteem and regard with which I am,
Sir, your very humble servant,

"PASQUALE DE PAOLI."

"CAPTN. WOLSELEY of the
Impérieuse."

It seems a pity that the writer of this letter
should have found his confidence in the English
Government was misplaced. But only two years
after the letter was written it was determined by
the Cabinet to evacuate Corsica. The Viceroy, Sir
Gilbert Elliot, was much dissatisfied at this decision,
and, as Dr. Southey writes, he "believed that the
great body of the Corsicans were perfectly satisfied,
as they had good reason to be, with the British
Government, sensible of its advantages, and attached
to it. However this may have been," the Doctor
adds, "when they found that the English intended
to evacuate the island, they naturally and necessarily
sent to make their peace with the French." Paoli
again took refuge in England, and died in London
on the 5th of February 1807. He was buried in
St. Pancras Churchyard, whence his remains were
removed on the 31st of August 1889 for transfer-
ence to his native land, where they were received
with great honours by his countrymen, who still
hold his efforts in the service of Corsica in grateful
recollection. A writer in the *St. James's Gazette*

of that period stated that " the committee who were appointed to carry out the exhumation of the remains of the famous Corsican general, Pasquale de Paoli —the friend of Dr. Johnson and of Goldsmith—were M. Franceschini Pietri (secretary of the Empress Eugénie), and the grandnephew and sole surviving relative of the illustrious patriot ; Count Benedetti (the ex-ambassador to Berlin before the Franco-German war) ; M. Ceccaldi, a Corsican deputy, and various other prominent representatives of the little Mediterranean island." And the writer added that M. Pietri had given the house at Stretta-de-Moro-salgia, in which Paoli was born, to the Department of Corsica, and that " the general's ashes were finally laid to rest by the side of those of his brother Clément, who had also fought during his whole life for the independence of his native isle."

G

CHAPTER V

DURING the time the negotiations were first going
on between General Paoli and Lord Hood about
the conquest of Corsica from the French, and also
in the interval between the sieges of St. Fiorenzo
and of Bastia, Captain Wolseley was employed in
a small squadron under Nelson in cruising in the
Mediterranean, for the purpose of keeping out all
supplies from Corsica, and intercepting despatches
and cutting-out vessels from the bay—"a species
of warfare," remarks Dr. Southey, "which depresses
the spirit of an enemy more than it injures them,
because of the sense of individual superiority which
it indicates in the assailants."

Captain Wolseley was at that time the only
officer who had the honour of sharing prize-money
with Lord Nelson; and three letters written by
the latter on the subject of this money are still
preserved among the papers left by Admiral
Wolseley. On the back of the first of these letters
there is this memorandum in the Admiral's handwriting :—

"I commanded the *Lowestoffe* frigate of 32
guns—and afterwards the *L'Impérieuse* frigate of

40 guns.   Nelson and I shared Prize-money ; he commanded the *Agamemnon* of 64 guns."

Unfortunately, a little piece of the paper the letter is written upon has been torn out, and a few words are missing :—

"*March 6th*, 1794.

"MY DEAR WOLSELEY, — have sent you your dagger.   I have sent a Ragusa vessel to Leghorn said to be very Rich hope she is, the account of the money is just come out I take for granted we share together write me if you wish it my offer at first was in hopes to have an opportunity of refunding what I had received, and if you like it the sharing shall go on till one [*word missing*] one month's notice.—Yours faithfully,   HORATIO NELSON.

" . . . I expect to be in action to-morrow if I am not active we shall lose Bastia."

The following is a copy of the second of these letters :—

"'AGAMEMNON,' LEGHORN, *Octr.* 28*th* 1794.

"MY DEAR WOLSELEY,—You will see I have not forgot my friends—but cash I have as yet touched none for you except 140 Tuscan crowns—the moiety of my little matter, which I will order Marsh and Creed to pay you 36£ sterling.   I only wish it had been more, at the Consuls I have left the acct.

which debits you a trifle, the officers of the *Lowestoffe* took all the proportion for the flour except yours, I have not finally settled that account. I send you Pollards account to me of the Privateer, you will not get half what you ought however its something—he hopes to touch the cash before I return and if he does I shall order him to remit it to my agent for I know not who are yours. the Condemnation is come out for the Swedish Brig taken by *Lowestoffe* off Toulon if enough is got to pay the expenses we shall be well off, the French frigates begin to be bold in the Mediterranean and have been cruizing off Gourjean Bay, in the absence of our fleet, very near taken the *Tarleton*, several of our vessels carried into Marseilles, out of which port they have 12 Brig and Polacco privateers. I shall be very glad to hear from you.—Believe me your most faithful friend,

"HORATIO NELSON.

"I have lost 50 men by the Calvi fever."

Third Letter.

"'AGAMEMNON,' ST. FIORENZA, *Febry. 1st* 1795.

"MY DEAR WOLSELEY,—I wrote you a line some time ago abt. your Corsican prize—and also directed my agents to pay you I think 35£ sterling which I hope they have done, Pollards Bill at that time brought you a few Zechinis in debt but he had not then given you credit for a Leuto taken off Caprea,[1] in the Consuls account there was a jumble about flour taken in the boat off Corsica, both these will be settled by the next time I go into Leghorn and I will send you the account, I know not what other vessels you share for and shall leave to you to pay my half of your receipt to my Agents. St. Fiorenza is not yet paid. You share of course for Bastia and Calvi as you was never out of service at both places. At Fiorenza I shall be a draw Back on you they will not let me share I dare say. I have at last got a letter telling me that Mr Tonnereau Mercht. at Leghorn will pay me for the Powder you landed at Calvi 168£ Sterling as soon as I get it will send the Bill home for the amount. the *Prince Royal* is in last condemned and but I hear a very small part. however be assured I will do my best to serve you. We are doing nothing worse than nothing last Cruize had 3 French Frigates under our Bows but the Adl. would not let us chase them and one a crippled ship and out of sight of land. You will have heard of the extraordinary event of the *Berwick* having rolled all her Masts away in the Bay for which the Captn. and 1st Lt. are dismissed the Ship and Master reprimanded. I have got old *Agamemnon* into tolerable order again and had I 50 good Men could do anything, but they are not to be had, I was in hopes lately of

[1] The island of Capraia, Mr. James mentions, is distant about thirty-six miles from Leghorn.

soon seeing England but they are at present much lessened and I fear will totally vanish, let me hear from you and what you are after. And Believe me ever your most sincere Friend,

" HORATIO NELSON.

" I passed young Boger for a Lieut. the other day and believe he stands some chance for a commission."

These three letters seem to have been written in great haste, and, as the reader will remark, there is scarcely a full stop in any one of them, and but few sentences are begun with a capital ; however, I thought it best to make no alteration, and they are consequently copied exactly as they are written.

The accident to the *Berwick*, alluded to by the celebrated sailor in the last letter, is also mentioned by Captain Brenton. It appears that it took place in Fiorenza Bay, which Captain Brenton speaks of as "a bad anchorage, and much exposed to the north-west winds, which send in a heavy sea." And he continues:—" The *Berwick*, of seventy-four guns, had her lower masts stripped without the proper precaution for securing them, by which neglect they rolled over the side. At no time could a ship of the line so ill be spared, and the admiral, conceiving that it had occurred from want of seamanship, directed the captain, first lieutenant, and master to be tried by a court-martial, when

they were all dismissed from the ship." This unfortunate accident led very soon afterwards to the
capture of the vessel by the French. And the
writer continues :—" In the meantime the fleet proceeded to Leghorn roads. The *Berwick* was left
under the command of Captain Littlejohn, to rig
jurymasts, and to follow as fast as possible ; and
having put to sea in pursuance of these orders,
with his ship as well equipped as circumstances
would admit, he fell in with the French fleet. A
running fight ensued, and every exertion was made
to save her ; but, after an ineffectual resistance, she
was forced to surrender, with the loss of her captain
and two or three of her men."

Towards the end of the year 1794 Captain
Wolseley returned to England. He says, in the
little memoir from which I have so frequently
quoted:—"*L'Impérieuse* was appointed to the convoy then going home (under Admiral Cosby, in
the *Windsor Castle*), which we carried in safe ; and
then *L'Impérieuse* was paid off, and it was understood that I was to be reappointed to a frigate,
under Lord Hood; but this appointment never took
place, and I went on half-pay."

In the beginning of the next year Captain
Wolseley wrote to Lord Hood for the purpose of
trying to get command of a vessel again, and the
following is his lordship's reply :—

"'VICTORY,' ST. HELENS, *April* 28, 1795.

" My DEAR WOLSELEY,—I have received your obliging letter of the 21st, for which I thank you, and have taken the liberty, which I have no right to do, to ask Lord Spencer to reappoint you to the *Impérieuse* and send you to the Mediterranean. And if I do not sail before I receive his answer you shall know it.—I am, my dear Wolseley, most faithfully your friend, HOOD."

Two days later Lord Hood sent a few lines to Captain Wolseley, with a copy he had taken of Lord Spencer's reply :—

"'VICTORY,' ST. HELENS, *April* 30, 1795.

" MY DEAR WOLSELEY,—Upon the receipt of your last letter expressing a wish to be reappointed to the *Impérieuse*, I took the liberty of writing to Lord Spencer in your favour, and underneath is his lordship's answer verbatim, which is all I can at present add, except that of being your faithful friend, HOOD.

" *Copy.*

" MY LORD,—Captain Wolseley has been some time down upon my list for a ship, when I can appoint him to one, consistently with my other engagements and your Lordship's recommendation of him will be a great additional inducement to me to wish that I may soon be enabled to do so ; with respect however to the frigate you mention she is already destined to Captn. Forbes, late of the *Southampton*, and I am consequently unable in this instance to pay that attention I could have wished to your Lordship's commands.—I have the honour to be, my Lord, your Lordship's most obedt. humble servant,   SPENCER.

"ADMIRALTY, 29*th April* 1795."

During his visit to Ireland in 1795, Captain Wolseley made the acquaintance of Miss Jane Moore, the youngest daughter of Mr. John Moore, of Clough House and Eglantine, in the county Down, and soon became much attached to her, as she was both very amiable and very beautiful. Her family was a branch of the very ancient Scottish house of Mure—or, as the name is sometimes spelt, Muir—of Rowallane. Her great-grandfather, Colonel Muir, an officer in the army of King William III., having obtained a grant of lands in Ulster, was the first of the family who settled in Ireland.

Captain Wolseley's marriage with Miss Jane Moore took place in the latter part of the year 1795; and as Mrs. Wolseley's father and mother were then living at Clough House, he took a little place in the neighbourhood, where he lived for a few years while he was unemployed. During that time he made several efforts to get employed on active service again, but without success. His old friend and commander, Lord Hood, was evidently not in a position to assist him in this object.

Captain Brenton mentions that, after the surrender of Calvi, Lord Hood returned to England in the month of November, leaving the temporary command of the fleet with Vice-Admiral Hotham ; but the latter shortly afterwards requested to be relieved from a responsibility to which his health was unequal, and it was arranged that Lord Hood should resume the chief command. "His lordship," writes Captain Brenton, "hoisted his flag on board the *Victory* at Spithead in the month of May [1795], and was about to sail to his station, when a correspondence ensued between the admiral and the new Board of Admiralty on the necessity of sending more ships to the Mediterranean. Lord Spencer, who was First Lord of the Admiralty at that time, thought that the force employed, if not sufficient, was as great as could be spared under the existing difficulties of the country, and the urgent demands of other parts of the empire.

"The admiral, not deeming his professional character safe with so small a force, expressed a very decided opinion upon the subject, and received permission to strike his flag, which he immediately did, and was never afterwards actively employed ; but as a reward for his long and meritorious services, and as a mark of his Majesty's approbation, he was appointed governor of Greenwich Hospital, which situation he held till his death, in 1816, at the great age of ninety-four years."

In the year 1796, about fourteen months after

the date of Lord Hood's last letter to him, Captain Wolseley was evidently again trying to get the command of a ship, and in answer to an application made to his lordship, received the following letter :—

"GREENWICH HOSPITAL, *August 2nd*, 1796.

" MY DEAR WOLSELEY,—I have been favoured with your letter of the 26th past and lose not a post to tell you so, that you may not leave Ireland with any hopes from me.

"Nothing would give me greater pleasure than to be able to assist your wishes in any respect whatever, as I not only esteem you as an honorable man, but as a gallant meritorious officer. But to be candid with you, I can be of no use to any one, for Lord Spencer is not content with marking me with indifference and inattention but carries it to all who have any connection with me ; you will therefore do well, in any application you may make to his Lordship, not to make mention of my name. I have neither seen or spoken to his Lordship since my flag was struck, and look upon myself as thrown upon the shelf for ever. It may be right it should be so. But a consciousness of having discharged my duty with zeal and industry, as a faithfull servant to the publick in the several situations in which I have had the honor to be placed, will bear me up against the treatment I have, and must ever think most undeservedly received, and will not fail to cheer my declining years. With every good wish for your Health and success in Life, I am most sincerely your faithfull humble servant, HOOD."

Apparently Lord Hood did not complain without reason of the treatment he had met with from the authorities at the Admiralty, for Captain Brenton says :—" As an ample justification of his demand, the ships which were refused to his application were granted to his successor, who, even with that augmentation, found himself unable to cope with the maritime power of France and Spain in the Mediterranean."

The warning given to Captain Wolseley by Lord Hood not to mention *his* name in any application for reappointment apparently came too late, as he had himself recommended Captain Wolseley to Lord Spencer's notice about a year before ; and despicable as such a motive for leaving a distinguished officer unemployed must appear to any generous-minded person, there can be no doubt that the subsequent quarrel with Lord Hood was the sole reason which prevented Lord Spencer from carrying out the intentions expressed by him in his letter of the 29th April 1795. Evidently this was Captain Wolseley's own opinion, for on the back of one of Lord Hood's letters to him is the following memorandum in his handwriting :—" These letters show the reason why I could not get employed between 1795 and 1799."

On the 3rd of October 1796, Captain Wolseley's eldest son, John Hood Wolseley, was born at Clough. In a letter dated October 22nd, evidently written in reply to a request of Captain Wolseley's, Lord Hood sends "all good wishes" to him and Mrs. Wolseley, and says :—"If my name to your new-born son can in any manner be gratifying to you, you are welcome to it, and this mark of your attention is as highly gratifying to me." He continues :—"I am sorry you have no better prospect of active employment. A little time, however, may produce many openings, for if we have not peace with France, which I am not at all sanguine can be brought about, a war with Spain must take place."

The position of affairs in the south of Europe towards the end of the year 1796, when Lord Hood's letter was written, is thus described by Captain Brenton. " Corsica," he writes, "was held only by the power of the sword, and the French were hourly on the alert to wrest it from us. The armies or the influence of the Republic now covered Italy from the Alps to Otranto, the King of Sardinia trembled for his throne, Naples was at their command, and the Grand Duke of Tuscany had no alternative but submission. There was no port in the Mediterranean which the English might safely enter but Gibraltar. . . . The enemy had a very large fleet at their disposal ; and the armies of the Republic having entered Spain on the side of Roussillon, her weak and corrupt Government was induced to abandon the coalesced powers, and at first secretly, and afterwards openly, to join itself to the murderers of Louis the Sixteenth and his unfortunate family. This disregard of her political interests and engagements," he adds, "was punished in the sequel both by France and England."

Under the circumstances thus described, it is not surprising that Lord Hood's prediction about a war with Spain was destined to be very speedily verified; and in the following year, on the 14th of February 1797, the great victory was gained in the battle fought off Cape St. Vincent, where Admiral Sir John Jervis defeated a Spanish fleet very much larger than his own, and thereby, as Captain Brenton remarks, added "fresh laurels to the maritime fame of Great Britain."

Evidently, from the passage quoted from Lord Hood's letter, Captain Wolseley was then still endeavouring to get appointed to the command of a vessel again, but, as already mentioned, without success; and the beginning of the year 1798, in which the dreadful insurrection known as the "Irish Rebellion of 1798" took place, found him and Mrs. Wolseley still living at the little place near Clough which he had taken after his marriage.

The state of affairs in the northern counties in the month of May 1798 is thus described by the writer of a "History of the Town of Belfast," published in 1823. "In May 1798," he writes, "martial law was proclaimed in the principal streets of this town, and four companies of yeomanry which had been formed here commenced regular duty, the activity of the Government and others increasing with the more certain tokens of the approaching insurrection. The brass field-pieces which had belonged to the volunteers were delivered to General Nugent, except one which was shortly after recovered from the rebels when they were defeated at Antrim. Sentinels were placed at the different outlets from the town, with rigid injunctions to permit no persons to pass except those coming to and from market. A number of the inhabitants were formed at the same time into a supplementary corps of yeomanry. When the rebellion broke out in the county of Down, many persons fled hither for security from different parts of the country; but several of them, fearing greater danger than the appearance of affairs really warranted, sailed from this port for England or Scotland."

Although the writer just quoted makes somewhat light of the dangers of the situation, an incident mentioned by the Rev. James Gordon, author of a "History of the Rebellion," published in 1803, proves that occasionally, at least, the rebels in the north might be expected to act with as great cruelty as those in the south. "In their progress through the country"—when on their way to Saintfield—he says, "they set fire to the house of a man named Mackie, who had been an informer of treasonable meetings.

Eleven persons perished in the flames amid circumstances of cruelty not inferior to those of the
burning at Scullabogue." And the following anecdote, told by Mrs. Wolseley many years afterwards
to her daughter, Mrs. Innes, shows that the dangers
to which people were exposed, who like herself
and her husband were at that time living in remote
country places, were both very real and very serious ;
and there cannot be the slightest doubt that, if
the insurrection in the northern counties had not
been very speedily put down, they would soon have
been the scene of similar atrocities to those per-
petrated by the rebels in Wexford and in other
parts of Ireland. When the rebellion first broke
out in Ulster, Captain Wolseley had in his service,
as footman, a man who was probably a member of
some secret society, but who was evidently attached
to his employers, and grateful for kindness he had
met with. This man one day came to Captain
Wolseley and begged him most earnestly to make
his arrangements about things he might require for
a journey, and implored him to leave the country,
and to lose no time, but to start at once. He said
that it had come to his knowledge that Captain
Wolseley's life was in very great danger, and told
him that his name was included in a list of gentlemen whom it was the intention of the rebels to
murder. He told Captain Wolseley that the night
when the crime was to be committed was not yet
fixed, but that, when it was, the plan was to break

into the house when the family were asleep; and he added that he must at once leave Captain Wolseley's service; that, if he remained, he would have to open the door to admit the murderers, and lead them to Captain Wolseley's room. He insisted on leaving at once, and said that, as it would cost him his own life if it was known that he had given Captain Wolseley this warning, he would have to tell every one about the place that he had been turned out of the house in disgrace; and, to give colouring to this story, he actually begged Captain Wolseley to take a whip, and to chase him with it down the short avenue which led up from the public road!

Although nothing appears to have been said about any danger to Mrs. Wolseley, it is most probable that she would have shared her husband's fate, if the wretches who thus deliberately planned his murder had succeeded in carrying out their wicked design. Her eldest brother, Captain Hugh Moore, of the 5th Dragoons, had raised, among the tenants on his father's estate, a company of volunteers, known by the name of " The Eglantine Yeomanry," of which he was the commander. He was also aide-de-camp to General Needham, who was at that time engaged, with the forces under his command, in putting down the insurrection in Wexford. These facts were probably well known to the country people living in the neighbourhood of Clough House; and in that case, judging

H

from the accounts of what had taken place elsewhere, it is scarcely likely that the assassins
would have spared the life of Captain Moore's
sister.

But, as a wise French saying runs, "*L'homme
propose, mais Dieu dispose*"; and a few weeks later
the revolutionists, utterly defeated in the town of
Antrim, at Portaferry, Saintfield, and Ballynahinch,
were powerless to carry out the plans of their
ringleaders, who were then either prisoners or fugitives from the country.

But for some time before affairs had arrived at
this point, the loyalists in every part of the north
were engaged in making preparations for defence,
in the event of a rising in Ulster.   Captain
Wolseley, by his exertions, succeeded in raising a
company of a hundred volunteers, and commanded
it himself in an engagement of some importance
that took place near the town of Ballynahinch, and
which has been dignified by all historians of the
Rebellion of '98 by the title of "the Battle of
Ballynahinch."

With bad news constantly arriving from other
parts of Ireland, and with disquieting rumours of
increasing disaffection in their own neighbourhood,
the last weeks before this engagement took place
must have been very anxious ones for people living
in isolated country places ; and Captain and Mrs.
Wolseley were very glad to accept an invitation
from the Dowager Lady Moira and her son, the

Earl of Moira, who very kindly asked them to come and stay with them until the country was more settled.[1]

On arriving at Moira House, Captain and Mrs. Wolseley found that hospitable mansion crowded with guests from different parts of the county, and among them were many friends of both, and also some relations of Mrs. Wolseley's. Under other circumstances the visit would have been a very pleasant one, but probably few people staying with Lord and Lady Moira at that time were able to enjoy it; for every one there must have been more or less anxious about the fate of relations at a distance, and perhaps afraid, too, that they might find their own homes wrecked when they returned to them, or that many things they valued might be either carried off or destroyed by the rebels. These latter, shortly before the battle of Ballynahinch, assembled in great force near that town, which is situated in a valley between a hill called the Windmill Hill and the high ground in Montalto, another demesne which then belonged to Lord Moira.[1]

[1] Francis Rawdon, second Earl of Moira, was in 1816 created Marquis of Hastings. He was Governor-General of India for some years. The Marquis, in 1804, married Flora Muir Campbell, Countess of Loudoun in her own right, whose mother was a descendant of the last Sir William Muir of Rowallan, and was heiress of that estate, which was in the possession of Mrs. Wolseley's ancestors as far back as the thirteenth century.

[2] Lord Moira had two places in the County Down—Moira House, where he was living at the time of the Rebellion, and Montalto,

The party at Moira House were for some days in a state of great anxiety, fearing that the rebels would come over there to attack them. Mrs. Wolseley and the other ladies were busily employed in making cartridges and lint, while the gentlemen were equally actively engaged in preparations for the defence of the house.

The following extract from a history of Ireland, published in the early part of this century, may be interesting to the reader. "Saintfield," the author says, "had become the principal rendezvous of the insurgents of Down, whose force assembled there on the 11th of June amounted at least to seven thousand men. Others have estimated their numbers at from eight to ten thousand. They proceeded to Ballinahinch, and established their camp, as they called it, in the demesne of Lord Moira, on a commanding eminence skirted with thick wood.[1]

"Requisitions were sent round to the gentry and small farmers for provisions, which were carried to them in considerable quantities. The son of one of the former accompanied his father's servants to the rebel camp, where he remained all night, and from his relation, published long afterwards in the *Belfast Magazine*, we have a curious account of the appear-

where the rebels established their camp. Montalto was afterwards sold to Mr. Ker, and Moira was bought by an ancestor of Lord Derramore.

[1] The name of the town is variously spelt by different writers, and sometimes as in the extract given above.

ance of the insurgents on this occasion. 'When
we arrived,' he says, 'there were on the ground
a considerable number of women, chiefly servants,
or the daughters or wives of cottiers or small
farmers. They were almost all employed on the
same business as ourselves, though it is said that
two or three of them remained on the field during
the night, submitting to their share of the labours
or dangers and performing as valiant deeds as the
men.

"'Nothing could surpass the delicacy and kindness with which these female visitors were received
and conducted through the camp. When those of
our party entered the field they were immediately
lightened of their burdens and escorted along with
them to a particular part of the ground, where the
provisions were placed under the care of persons
appointed to receive and distribute them, and two
or three young men offered their services to conduct
us through the field. Everything was explained
with minuteness; pikes of different constructions
were pointed out and their uses explained; the
cannon and ammunition were shown, and the tremendous effects glanced at which they were calculated to produce. The leaders were also pointed
out, the more distinguished and the greater favourites among them with pride and exultation. A
mixed and motley multitude met the eye, some
walking about, others stretched listlessly on the
green turf or along the field, a considerable

number sheltering themselves from the scorching
sun under the shade of the trees with which
the field was skirted, and many sleeping on the
grass.

"'They wore no uniform, yet they presented
a tolerably decent appearance, being dressed, no
doubt, in their Sunday clothes; some better and
some worse, but none in the ragged costume that
is often to be seen in other parts of Ireland. The
only thing in which they all concurred was the
wearing of the green, almost every individual
having a knot of ribbons of that colour, sometimes
intermixed with yellow, in his hat. Most of them,
besides, had their hats and button-holes decorated
with laurel from the adjoining grounds. The
leaders in general wore green or yellow belts, and
some of them green coats; and those under their
command bore decorations of various descriptions,
and of different degrees of taste and execution.
The most common of the decorations was the harp
entwined with shamrock or bays, but without the
crown; the British lion and unicorn in a falling
attitude; and many other symbolic representations,
with various corresponding inscriptions expressive
of the wishes and feelings of the people, such as
"Liberty or death," "Downfall to tyrants," "Freedom to Ireland," and many others of a similar
character.

"'In their arms there was as great a diversity as
in their dress. By far the majority of them had

pikes, which were truly formidable instruments in close fight, but of no use in distant warfare. These had generally wooden shafts seven feet long with sharpened heads of steel of different forms, and commonly ten or twelve inches long ; some of these heads consisted simply of one longitudinal piece, but others had another piece crossing this and forming a sort of hook, which was thought. likely to be of use in cutting the bridles of their opponents' horses. Others wore old swords, generally of the least efficient kind, and some had merely pitchforks. Those of the higher class were armed with guns. There were also seven or eight pieces of small cannon mounted on common cars, which, however, did not seem calculated to produce much effect.'"

The rebel commander-in-chief was a man named Henry Munro, a shopkeeper of Lisburn, and the forces under him seem to have been collected from all parts of the counties of Down and Antrim. Mr. Maxwell, in his " History of the Irish Rebellion in 1798," says that after Munro had been unanimously elected their commander "a large body of insurgents entered Bangor and compelled numbers to join them. Proceeding to Saintfield, they joined the body that held that town, and on the next morning, Monday, 11th of June, the whole proceeded to the rebel camp at Ballynahinch, where the insurgent headquarters were established."

On the morning of the 12th, General Nugent,

the general in command of the northern district,
marched from Saintfield.   The force under him,
according to some accounts, consisted of about 1500
men ; or, as Mr. Maxwell says, the Royalists, after
they had been joined by Lieutenant-Colonel Stewart,
with the garrison of Downpatrick, "mustered probably 1600 men, with eight pieces of light artillery."
General Nugent's army consisted of the Monaghan
Militia regiment, part of the 22nd Dragoons, the
Hillsborough and other yeomanry corps, both horse
and foot ; and among the latter, who are not more
particularly specified, was included a company of a
hundred volunteers which were raised and commanded by Captain Wolseley.

The statement made by the author previously
quoted, of the strength of the insurgents encamped
at Montalto, shows that they far outnumbered the
small army opposed to them ; but the latter had the
advantage of being better armed, and of being led
by experienced officers.   In his "History of the
Irish Rebellion" Mr. Maxwell gives a very amusing
account of some circumstances which apparently
prevented Munro from getting a considerable
addition to his forces at Ballynahinch.   The two
anecdotes, I think, may find a place here, especially
as the incident he mentions last occurred at Innishargy, the residence of Mr. Baillie, a cousin of
Mrs. Wolseley's.

"When Down caught the flame of rebellion,"
writes Mr. Maxwell, "a body of insurgents as-

sembled in the barony of Ards, and moved on Portaferry. Their object was, on taking that town, to have crossed the ferry and proceeded, with whatever aid they could get in Lecale, to the attack of Downpatrick. The plan showed some head; for the presumption was, that the garrison of Downpatrick would either have marched—as was the case—to co-operate with General Nugent at Ballynahinch, or that the rebel approach from the Portaferry side would keep it still in Downpatrick. In the former case, the town would be open to them; in the latter, General Nugent would have been deprived of the assistance of the garrison. The yeomanry of Portaferry, however, gave matters a different turn.

"When this body of rebels was on their way to that place, they halted, about a mile from the town, at a large and well-stored public-house. Here they ordered out all the house contained, and eatables and drinkables rapidly disappeared. I must give," continues Mr. Maxwell, "what followed in the words of my informant, who was brother to the man of the house, and one of the rebel 'airmy,' as he called it :—' My brither cam' out quite civil, and "Wha's to pay *me*, gentlemen?" quoth he. "Hoot, man!" says ane, and "Hoot, man!" says anither, "your country will pay you." My brither gied a look at me, and I at him, as they moved on; and from that time I thought I had been lang enoo' in the airmy, so I slipped behind the dyke, and let

them gang on without me. And weel it was I did
sae; for afore twa hours' time they were back again,
far faster than they went, and not all of them either.
But not ae word did my brither hear o' the reck'nin'
frae that hour to this. Aweel, sir, the King's men,
whether sodgers or sailors, always paid decently ;
so I'll e'en stick to them.' "

Mr. Maxwell continues :—" The discomfited insurgents then made their way to the residence of
Mr. Baillie of Innishargy, five or six miles along
the shore of the lough, from the scene of their
defeat. Here, as my informant, another of the
party, thus described their proceedings, 'the airmy
lay down on the lawn, while the affishers took possession of the house, and having made themselves
free of the cellar, sat down in the parlour, enjoying
themselves wi' the best it afforded. With that, my-
sel' and ane or twa mair of us made up to the open
window, and "Merry be yer hearts, gentlemen,"
says we, "and what'll ye ha'e the airmy to drink?"
"Hoot!" says this ane and that ane, "there's a
water-cart in the yard; tak' it down to the river,
and fill enough for the people to drink." "Hech,
sirs!" says we, "is that the way of it? Gin we're
aye to be *soles* and ye *uppers*, in that fashion, we
may as weel serve King George as the likes o' ye!"
An' in five minutes, sir, the hale airmy had melted
away like snaw aff a dyke.'" And Mr. Maxwell
adds :—" Now, these were lessons which neither
sabre nor bayonet could teach, and particularly to

cannie northerns. The consequence was, that these
men not only abandoned the standard of rebellion,
but numbers of them actually joined a yeomanry
corps."

I must now return to the rebels assembled at
Lord Moira's place, near Ballynahinch, taking my
account of their proceedings partly from Mr. Maxwell's "History of the Rebellion," and partly from
the "History of Ireland" previously mentioned.
"Munro," on his arrival at Ballynahinch, according
to the author of the latter work, "made his military
arrangements with considerable skill." He sent a
part of his force to take possession of the town,
which lies in a valley, having on the north the
Windmill Hill, and on the south the commanding
eminence of Montalto, forming, with its plantations,
a very strong position. With the rest of his followers, Munro continued to occupy the heights
surrounding the town. On the 12th of June he
stationed a strong force at Creevy Rocks, near
Saintfield, to oppose the march of the troops under
General Nugent, and placed a party of his best
musketeers, under a leader named M'Cance, in
ambuscade, on an advantageous position at Windmill Hill, about a quarter of a mile from the town of
Ballynahinch. The King's troops "easily dispersed
the insurgents posted at Creevy Rocks, but they met
with more resistance at Windmill Hill. M'Cance,"
the author continues, "who displayed the most
extraordinary courage and considerable military

skill, kept the army in check for upwards of an
hour." But General Nugent, as Mr. Maxwell
writes, "drove those who occupied the Mill Hill
from it, and hung up one of the leaders, who was
too late in escaping with his men to the opposite
height of Montalto." It was then late in the afternoon, and Munro withdrew his men from the town,
and also all his outposts; and General Nugent
occupied the Windmill Hill that night.

With the great superiority of numbers on
Munro's side, consisting of a force said to have
been "certainly not less than seven thousand men,"
and that probably was nearer ten thousand, to oppose General Nugent's small army of 1500 or 1600
men, it seemed to Munro that defeat in the engagement that was inevitable next day would be quite
an impossibility. And so certain was he of success
that, as Mr. Maxwell says, "late on the evening of
the 12th, in a hasty despatch from his bivouac on
Lord Moira's lawn, Munro declared 'that victory was
certain, and the British army was within his grasp.'
This idle vaunt," continues Mr. Maxwell, "was
communicated to the station selected as the rallying
point for the central division, . . . and Munro's
rank folly," he adds, "annihilated the last chances
and the last hopes of the disaffected," as it effectually prevented the party to whom the message
was sent from joining him at Ballynahinch. The
majority having decided, according to Mr. Maxwell,
that it was best "to wait the issue of the night,

and then to press for the important post of Newry,"
as the most "important advantages were to be
obtained by the capture of a garrison town, commanding from its local situation the key of the
province. . . . With the morrow," he adds,
"came the astounding intelligence of Munro's
defeat! And in the general panic which succeeded
few were bold enough even to entertain the idea
of offering further resistance."

The chief incidents of the rebel campaign in
Ulster were the attacks upon Antrim, Portaferry,
and Saintfield, and the final and most important
engagement, the so-called " Battle of Ballynahinch,"
at which Captain Wolseley was present, and commanded the little corps of a hundred volunteers
which he had succeeded in raising ; and doubtless,
as the regular troops were so few in number, this
little company, with the advantage of being led by
an officer of Captain Wolseley's experience, gave
some valuable assistance, as General Nugent's very
small army was at first repulsed and nearly swept
away by the overpowering masses of the rebels,
who, by all accounts, fought with the greatest
courage.

The following particulars of the battle are given
by the author of the " History of Ireland," previously quoted, and by the Rev. James Gordon.
" Early in the morning of the 13th of June," writes
the author first mentioned, "the rebel general
commenced the action by a discharge of eight

small pieces of cannon, which was replied to by
the heavy artillery of the army; but though this
cannonade continued for some time, it did no great
hurt on either side." This fact is fully explained by
Mr. Gordon, who says :—"The cannon of the insurgents were small and tied on the backs of cars, while
the shells thrown from the mortars of the Royal
army were furnished with too short fuses, so that
they burst in the air."

Mr. Gordon continues :—"The Monaghan regiment of militia, posted with two field-pieces at Lord
Moira's great gate, was attacked with such determined fury by the pikemen of the insurgents that
it fell back in great confusion on the Hillsborough
cavalry, who likewise fell back in equal disorder.
But the want of discipline of the insurgents caused
the loss of what their valour had gained." And
he adds :—"The disordered troops found means
to rally while the Argyleshire fencibles, entering
the demesne, were making an attack on another
side."

The fighting, apparently, was kept up with the
greatest determination both by the loyalist forces
and by the rebels for a considerable time. And
the author of the "History of Ireland" says :—
"At length one division of the insurgents made
an attempt to penetrate into the town, while
Munro, at the head of the remainder of his force,
attacked the main body of the King's troops.
Munro's men charged with the utmost courage,

drove their opponents back, and made their way into the town, though exposed to a shower of musketry and grape shot, which swept away whole ranks of the insurgents. At the market square, in the centre of the town, the struggle was for a short time very obstinate, and the efforts of the rebels were so great that General Nugent judged it necessary to withdraw his troops from the town. The sound of the bugle for the retreat is said to have been mistaken by the rebels, who imagined that it announced the arrival of new troops for a renewal of the combat, and they were in consequence seized with a sudden panic and fled in confusion.

"For a moment the town was evacuated by both parties, and then the King's troops, rallying, charged through it and pursued the insurgents, who were flying up the hill of Ednavady. Munro attempted to rally them at the top, where a stand was made in some ancient entrenchments; but the hill being now almost surrounded by the King's troops, he led off the small force that still remained with him, which is said not to have exceeded a hundred and fifty men, through the only opening that afforded him a retreat."

"A general dispersion ensued," writes Mr. Maxwell, "and the rebels were totally routed, leaving four hundred men *hors de combat*." This, of course, included both killed and wounded. As the author of the History remarks, "the slaughter in this engagement appears to have been much less than might have been expected. The King's troops lost about forty, and the rebels are said to have lost in the fight not more than a hundred and fifty men. But," the writer adds, "their loss in the flight was much greater." This statement, however, appears to be a great exaggeration, and is not borne out by other writers, or by Mr. Maxwell, who says :—" Many were saved from the nature of the country, which, being wooded and uneven, was unfavourable to the action of the cavalry ; others owed their escape to accidental circumstances."

The rebel leader, Munro, attempted to escape towards the mountains, but, writes Mr. Maxwell, "he was speedily detected by some Royalists, concealed in a potato furrow under some loose litter in an open field five or six miles distant from the scene of his folly and defeat. On being apprehended," the unfortunate man " endeavoured," Mr. Maxwell adds, "to bribe his captors and obtain his liberty. But he was brought into Hillsborough, and afterwards transmitted to Lisburn, tried by court-martial on the next Friday, and paid the penalty of his treason with his life."

The other writers state that "the main party of the fugitives from Ballynahinch fled to the mountains of Slieve-Croob, where they soon dispersed and returned to their homes." And thus ended the revolt in the north, which Mr. Maxwell speaks of as "a weak attempt at revolution"! but which is certainly more accurately, though perhaps somewhat more quaintly, described by Mr. Gordon as a "very short and partial, but active and vigorous insurrection."

CHAPTER VI

As soon as any fear of a further rising in the nor-thern province appeared to be over, and the country seemed a little more settled, the party that were assembled at Moira House broke up, and Captain and Mrs. Wolseley took leave of their kind friends, Lord and Lady Moira, and returned to their little place near Clough.

The remaining months of the memorable year 1798 passed away without bringing any change in Captain Wolseley's position. But in the early part of 1799 he was appointed to the *Terrible*, seventy-four guns, attached to the Channel fleet under Lord Bridport.

"In the first three months of the year," before Captain Wolseley was appointed to the command of that vessel, according to Mr. James, "the British force cruising off Brest consisted of a squadron of eight or nine sail of the line, under the successive command of Vice-Admiral Sir Charles Thompson, Bart., Vice-Admiral Sir Hugh Seymour, and Rear-Admiral the Honourable George Berkeley. On the 16th of April a French convoy was chased by Admiral Berkeley's squadron, but effected their escape into Brest."

On the 13th, Admiral Lord Bridport, in his flag-
ship the *Royal George*, 100 guns, and with five or
six other ships—the *Terrible* among the number—
sailed from St. Helens, and on the 17th, early
in the morning, arrived off Ushant, and superseded
Rear-Admiral Berkeley in the command.   Mr.
James gives a list of the ships at that time in the
Channel fleet, from which it appears that, besides
his flag-ship, already mentioned, Lord Bridport had
under his command four 98-gun ships, one 80 and
ten 74-gun ships, and included among the latter
he mentions " the *Terrible*, commanded by Captain
William Wolseley "; and he adds, "making in all
sixteen sail of the line, with three or four frigates,
of which the names are not given."

"On the evening of the 25th of April," writes
Mr. James, "the French fleet sailed from Brest."
This fleet, he remarks, was one of the largest ever
sent to sea by the French ; the ships had enormous
crews, and many of them were employed as transports, with a very large military force on board.
The fleet consisted of one 120-gun ship, three 110-
gun ships, two 80-gun ships, and nineteen 74-gun
ships, making in all, he says, "twenty-five ships
of the line, besides five frigates and five smaller
vessels."

"It was about 9 A.M. on the 26th," he continues,
"just as the last ten or eleven ships of this immense
fleet were rounding the Saintes, that the British
36-gun frigate, *Nymphe*, Captain Percy Fraser, dis-

covered them. Making all sail to rejoin her fleet with the intelligence, the *Nymphe*, at noon—Ushant being distant five leagues—lost sight of the French ships, and at 1 P.M., with the signal for an enemy flying, fell in with the *Dragon*, who quickly repeated the signal to Lord Bridport's fleet. The admiral immediately made sail towards Brest, and found that the French fleet had really eluded his vigilance." Lord Bridport, thinking it was their intention to attempt another invasion of Ireland, at once set sail for Cape Clear, where he arrived on the 30th, and where the reinforcements ordered to join him augmented his fleet to twenty-six sail of the line.

As all readers of the history of the Rebellion of 1798 are, of course, aware, the rising in Ireland in that year had scarcely been put down, when the French Government, for the purpose of assisting the rebels, sent over a force which landed at Killala, on the coast of Mayo. But that a fresh invasion of Ireland was contemplated in the year 1799 seems to have been doubtful. At all events none took place then, although, as Mr. James writes, "the Paris journals persisted in declaring that Ireland was the destination of the French armament." And he says:—"Among the smaller vessels that joined Lord Bridport was the hired armed lugger, *Black Joke*, which, when twenty leagues west of Ushant, had fallen in with and captured the French *chasse-marée*, *Rebecca*, of four swivels and seven men, just out of Brest, having on board a *capitaine de frégate* with despatches for Ireland." This, Mr. James adds, "was, of course, a ruse ; and a successful one it proved, as it fixed the British admiral to the Irish coast."

Captain Brenton, in his "Life and Correspondence of John, Earl of St. Vincent," commenting on a letter written at that time by Lord St. Vincent to Earl Spencer, in which the former mentions the arrival of the French fleet in the Mediterranean on the 5th May, says :—"It would seem that Lord Keith had nearly brought the enemy within sight of his fleet, and had he done so a tremendous conflict would probably have anticipated the great day of Trafalgar. Napoleon had united the two fleets of France and Spain, by the sailing of the former from Brest in the month of April. They picked up the Spanish division at Cadiz, then pushed for Carthagena, where they were equally successful in getting out the ships from that port. The French admiral seems then to have fulfilled the utmost letter of his instructions, for Buonaparte apparently had wisely forbidden him to fight. This was the finest fleet the enemy ever had at sea, and they had the good fortune to get safe back to Brest."

Captain Brenton adds :—"Had Napoleon ever seriously thought of invasion, this was his time ; but the fact is, he never seriously did intend it. If he had, he had only to have kept his combined fleet ready for sea, and made an indication of sailing, while the flotilla from Boulogne, Havre, and the Helder had embarked the army." No event of any consequence occurred during the rest of the time Captain Wolseley served under Lord Bridport; and towards the end of the year Lord St. Vincent was appointed to the command of the Channel fleet—"a situation," Captain Brenton remarks, "by no means enviable at that particular period, the ships being now worn and in want of repair; the crews dissatisfied with the long continuance of the war and the dull monotony of the blockade, unbroken, except very rarely, by any accident of capture, still less of battle; for the enemy had got so wary since the destruction of their fleet at the Nile that they never showed themselves at sea, unless in such a force as we have just related to have escaped into Brest."

In the spring of 1800 Lord Bridport had the command of the Channel fleet until Lord St. Vincent, who, on account of failing health, had been on leave for a few months, returned to take it again. And Captain Brenton says :—" His lordship hoisted his flag in his favourite ship, the *Ville de Paris*, which, having been sent home and properly repaired, was ready to receive him; and he took his station off Ushant, with the hope that the combined fleets, which we have seen in the preceding year escape into Brest, would come out and try their strength with him. But in this he was disappointed; and in the month of May the fleet was driven into Torbay by one of the most tremendous hurricanes," Captain Brenton continues, "that I ever remember. It came on during the night of the 16th and 17th, and blew with a violence which was never witnessed by the oldest seaman. The *Ville de Paris* scudded before it, and I am told," he says, "by those who were on board of her, that her motion was awful. Lord St. Vincent was seated in an arm-chair, lashed on one side of the quarter-deck, and thence gave his orders. The fleet, however, arrived without much damage in Torbay, which, with the wind in the position it then was (between west and south-west), offered a most friendly and acceptable shelter."

But the writer adds :—" During the hurricane two unfortunate sloops of war, the *Trompeuse* and the *Railleur*, were turned bottom up, and all on board perished. These vessels," he says, "were of that vile French corvette class, with weak upper works and flush decks, run up with slight materials, made for sailing mostly in light winds, but never calculated to meet the weather of our climate. They were usually built at Bordeaux, Morlaix, or St. Malo, on speculation ; and a desperate specu- lation it was. They made, perhaps, two or three captures of some value before they were taken by our active cruisers, in which case the owners were amply repaid. On the other hand, if they were taken soon after they left their port, which was very frequently the case, the loss was divided by insurance among so many shareholders as to be of little importance."

The same author remarks that "the year 1800 was comparatively quiet within the circle of Lord St. Vincent's command," and "in consequence," he says, "there were few incidents in it worth recording." But another naval historian, Dr. Campbell, gives the following slight sketch of the operations of the navy in that year, and also some details of the services performed by the division of the fleet commanded by Lord St. Vincent, in which division, it will be remembered, Captain Wolseley was then serving.

"As the British Ministry," Dr. Campbell writes, "had formed a regular combination on the Continent against the power of France, they were resolved to give the Royalists and their other allies every assistance which our navy was capable of affording. The Austrians being employed in the siege of Genoa, a detachment of men-of-war was ordered to assist them, and was of great use during the operations of the siege. That the French might not be able to send reinforcements to Genoa, Toulon was blockaded. Alexandria, Cadiz, Flushing, Malta, and Belleisle were also blockaded nearly at the same time by British fleets or cruisers. The whole coast of Europe, from Holland to the extremity of the Mediterranean, was thus held in check by the navy of England, and terror was inspired into our enemies by the names of St. Vincent, Nelson, Smith, and Mitchell. Such is a rapid and general sketch," Dr. Campbell adds, "of the services of the British navy in the year 1800." And he continues :—

"As the Royalists on the coast of Brittany had again appeared in strength, and expressed a wish to be assisted by the British, Lord St. Vincent, in the month of June, despatched Sir Edward Pellew,[1] with a squadron of ships of war, having a considerable body of troops on board, on this service. Major-General Maitland had the command of the land forces. Quiberon and the Bay of Morbihan were the places where the Royalists were in the greatest force, and where it was supposed a landing and co-operation might be effected with the greatest ease and success. But this enterprise was not attended with any important or permanent success. This was owing entirely to the circumstance of the Royalists being much less formidable than they had represented themselves to be. The forts on the south-west end of Quiberon were silenced and destroyed ; several vessels were cut out and captured ; but this is nearly the sum total of the result of this expedition.

"As so little could be done at Quiberon, Sir Edward Pellew and General Maitland resolved to make an attack on Belleisle. If this had been done

[1] Afterwards Viscount Exmouth, Vice-Admiral of England, 1831. Died 1833.

as soon as the plan was matured, it probably would
have succeeded; but some delay took place from
unforeseen circumstances; the enemy were alarmed
and prepared; and on the morning of the 19th of
June, General Maitland received information that a
body of troops, amounting to 7000, were assembled
on the island. Nothing now could be done against
Belleisle; the small island of Houatt was, indeed,
taken possession of for a short time, but this also
was abandoned, and the troops proceeded to the
Mediterranean, where, it was thought, they might
be more serviceably employed.

"If we look at this attempt on the coast of
France," Dr. Campbell continues, "solely with
reference to the assistance and support which it
might have given to the Royalists, we shall be
disposed to regard it as having utterly failed; but
if it is viewed as a measure intended to distract the
attention of the enemy, it had no slight degree of
success. At the time, when the coasts of France
were kept in constant alarm, it was of the utmost
importance for the French Government to send all
the troops they could spare against their Continental
foes; this, undoubtedly, they were prevented from
doing by our expedition, and so far the design was
good and the result beneficial."

Towards the end of the year the fleet were
again in Torbay; and, I believe, about that time
the place near Clough where Captain and Mrs.
Wolseley had been previously living was given

up, and Mrs. Wolseley came over to Torquay, so as to be near her husband, whose ship, the *Terrible*, was then stationed in the bay with the rest of the Channel fleet.

In a letter to the Earl of St. Vincent, written on board the *Terrible*, and dated December 4, 1800, Captain Wolseley says :—" Not being able to summon sufficient assurance (tho' so long resident in Ireland), to mention the subject of this letter to your Lordship when I had the honour of seeing you yesterday, I therefore take the liberty of troubling you at present. Having heard in various ways that a promotion will soon take place, I presume some of the 2d rates may thereby be vacant; and tho' I have no claim on your Lordship, but that of the honour of being under your command, I have to request that your Lordship will be pleased to intercede with Earl Spencer to appoint me to one of the 2d rates; should it not break in on any of your arrangements."

In reply to this, Captain Wolseley received the following very gratifying note from the Earl :—

" TOR ABBEY, *Dec. 5th*, 1800."

" SIR, — Your well established reputation and' excellent conduct since you have been under my command, give you a just claim to every possible attention and regard I can show ; and I will represent your wishes in the strongest manner to Lord Spencer by this day's post; and take the earliest opportunity to apprize you of the success of my application, being with much esteem very sincerely yours,   " ST. VINCENT.

"To CAPTAIN WOLSELEY, *Terrible.*"

In consequence of Lord St. Vincent's recommendation, Captain Wolseley was nominated to the *St. George,* ninety-eight guns. But in the following year, 1801, Lord Nelson, when on the point of sailing for Copenhagen, gave his own ship, the fine three - decker, *San Josef,* 112 guns, to Captain Wolseley, and removed his flag to the *St. George,* on account of its being a vessel of lighter draught of water than the *San Josef,* to which, by *express request* of Lord Nelson, Captain Wolseley was then duly appointed.

Lord Nelson, however, did not gain his fresh laurels on board of the *St. George,* and Captain Brenton gives the following account of his exchange of that vessel for the *Elephant,* in which he fought the famous battle of Copenhagen. "Nelson, it will be remembered," writes Captain Brenton, "was appointed second in command in the Copenhagen expedition in 1801, Sir Hyde Parker having the command-in-chief. Soon after the fleet came to an anchor off the entrance of the sound, between the castles of Cronenbourg and Helsinbourg, but out of gun-shot from either the Swedes or the Danes, the commander-in-chief received intelligence from the shore which induced him to pause, conceiving, from the report, that the enemy was lying in eighteen feet water, and that it would be impossible for our ships of the line to approach within sufficient distance to attack them with any reasonable prospect of success. It blew hard, and there was a good deal of sea running, when Nelson received a message from Sir Hyde signifying that, as he (the admiral) perceived there was no chance of succeeding in their attack on Copenhagen, he had decided upon returning to England.

" Nelson determined to wait upon the admiral immediately, and he desired Captain Hardy, of the *St. George*, on board which ship he then was, to have a boat manned for him to go on board the *London*, the commander-in-chief's ship. The captain expressed a doubt of his lordship's being able, with the sea that was running, and his having but one arm, to get into the boat. ' But I am determined I will go,' said Nelson. ' Then,' said Hardy, ' I must put you into the boat as she lays on the booms, and hoist you out in her.' This was accordingly done, with every proper and seaman-like precaution, and a boat's crew of the very best seamen was chosen. Thus away went Nelson, with the view to obtain the sanction of his superior to make the attempt with the smallest ships of the line, assisted by the frigates and all the small vessels of the fleet. After much discussion, the permission he so anxiously desired was

granted, although Sir Hyde still seemed to think
the attempt would be useless or unsuccessful.
Nelson then shifted his flag to the *Elephant*, and
proceeded to the attack." And, as Captain Brenton
remarked before telling this anecdote of our great
naval hero, "Nelson, when the enemy was in
sight, was never eclipsed. He never permitted
any one to stand between him and his glory; and
the battle of Copenhagen and its results are well
known."

The two naval historians, Mr. James and Captain
Brenton, both speak in the highest terms of the
Spanish first-rate, the *San Josef*, the splendid ship
to which, by particular request of Lord Nelson,
Captain Wolseley had recently been appointed. It
was one of the two ships of war captured by Nelson
from the Spaniards in the battle fought off Cape
St. Vincent on the 14th February 1797, and is
stated by Mr. James, who gives the dimensions of
both vessels, to have been superior in size to the
Ville de Paris, previously the largest ship in the
British navy.

Another writer gives the following interesting
account of the capture of the *San Nicolas*, of eighty
guns, and the *San Josef*, of one hundred and
twelve. "After engaging the Spanish four-decker,
Santissima Trinidad," he writes, "Commodore
Horatio Nelson directed the fire of his ship, the
Captain, against the *San Nicolas*. This ship ran
foul of and entangled herself with the *San Josef*.

The *Captain* lost her fore-topmast, and Nelson, fearing that she would drop astern, ran her into the starboard quarter of the *San Nicolas.*

"A private of the 69th, a regiment then acting as marines, broke in the windows of the upper starboard-quarter gallery of the *San Nicolas,* and was immediately followed by Nelson, whose triumphant exclamation of 'Westminster Abbey or victory!' was received by a ringing British cheer from the boarding party which was closely following him. The ship was soon taken, and apparently, from the circumstance of Nelson's having passed over her to take possession of the *San Josef,* it was afterwards, as he mentions in one of his letters, styled in the fleet, 'Nelson's patent bridge for boarding first-rates;' a saying, he remarks, 'too flattering for me to omit telling.'

"On the surrender of the *San Nicolas,* Nelson pushed forward and led the boarders over the bulwarks of the *San Josef,* and he and his brave followers quickly overcame the resistance offered to them. At this moment a Spanish officer called from the quarter-deck rail that the ship had surrendered, and the swords of the admiral and other officers were immediately afterwards given up to Nelson. The incident is thus described in his own words :—'On the quarter-deck of a Spanish first-rate, extravagant as the story may seem, did I receive the swords of vanquished Spaniards, which as I received I gave to William Fearney,

one of my bargemen, who put them, with the
greatest *sang froid*, under his arm. I was surrounded by Captain Berry, Lieutenant Pearson,
of the 69th Regiment, John Sykes, John Thomson,
Francis Cooke, all old *Agamemnons*, and several
other brave men, seamen and soldiers. Thus
fell these ships.' In a postscript he adds :—
'In boarding the *San Nicolas* I believe we
lost about seven killed and ten wounded, and
about twenty Spaniards lost their lives by a
foolish resistance. None were, I believe, lost in
boarding the *San Josef.*'"

Captain Brenton, in his "Life of the Earl
of St. Vincent," remarks that "in the art of
constructing ships of war the French were a
full century ahead of us." And he continues :—
"It is also well known that in almost every
instance when ships of war have been taken
from the enemy they have become favourites
in our service." He then gives, as proofs of
the truth of this assertion, a list of vessels taken
from the French, and adds at the end of the
long roll of names, "and finally, those *ne plus
ultras* of naval construction, *San Josef* (Spanish),
Tonnant, *Malta*, and *Canopus* (French), taken in
1797 and 1798." Of the first of these *especially*
highly praised vessels he says in his "Naval
History":—"The *San Josef*, of one hundred and
twelve guns, taken in the battle off Cape St.
Vincent, in 1797, was long admired in the British

navy, uniting all the superior qualities of a ship of the line with the sailing of the fastest frigate; her lower deck ports were higher with all her sea-stores in than was ever known in any other ship of the line, and she could carry her guns run-out when few British ships would have ventured to open a port; she stowed 600 tons of water, and," he adds, "we had nothing that could be compared to her as a ship of war.

Mr. James gives the dimensions of the vessel, which was a three-decker of 2457 tons, in his "Naval History," and says that "the crew of the *San Josef*, including men and boys, at the time she was captured, as far as could be ascertained, consisted of nine hundred and seventeen." And it may interest the reader to know that the length of the first gun-deck of this "the largest ship then in the British navy" is stated by him to have been "194 feet 3 inches, and the extreme width 54 feet 3 inches."

Apparently Lord St. Vincent considered the *San Josef* a good model for the size of a first-rate man-of-war, as he says in a letter written by him to Rear-Admiral Markham in 1806:—"I hope you will never build a seventy-four larger than the *Impétueux* or *Donegal*, nor a first-rate beyond the *Ville de Paris* and *St. Joseph*."[1]

[1] The *San Josef* was broken up in 1849, by order of the Board of Admiralty. It was for many years before that, when considered unfit for further service at sea, stationed off Greenwich, and was

Captain Wolseley had the honour of commanding this celebrated ship from the beginning of
the year 1801 until the signature of the Peace of
Amiens. Until the end of the year 1801 he was
employed in cruising with the Channel fleet off
Ushant, under Admiral the Honourable William
Cornwallis, who, on the 21st of February, had succeeded the Earl of St. Vincent as Commander-in-
Chief, in consequence of Lord St. Vincent having
been appointed First Lord of the Admiralty.

On the 7th July in the same year Captain
Wolseley's eldest surviving daughter was born
at Torquay. A few months later, the Channel
fleet being again in the bay, the child was
christened at the old church, known, I believe,
as " Tor Church," and Admiral Lord St. Vincent
was her godfather.[1]

A most gratifying proof of Captain Wolseley's
popularity with the sailors under his command
was given by them on that occasion. Having
requested leave to be present at the ceremony,
every one who could be spared from the ship
appeared at the church, which was crowded with
officers and seamen from the *San Josef.* On the

used as a convalescent hospital for sailors. Some interesting relics
of the old ship were to be seen in the great Naval Exhibition of
1891.

[1] Admiral and Mrs. Wolseley had another daughter, who, I think,
was born previously, but she died at the age of seven. Mary Jervis
Wolseley, mentioned above, married Arthur Innes, J.P. and D.L.,
of Dromantine, County Down. Mrs. Innes survived her husband,
and died at an advanced age in 1886.

arrival of Captain and Mrs. Wolseley and some friends they had invited, they formed a guard of honour ready to receive them at the church door—the sailors drawn up in lines on one side, and the marines on the other; and when the men came out of church after the ceremony was over, they formed a long procession, walking in twos and twos after the carriages. They escorted the christening party to Captain and Mrs. Wolseley's villa, where they dispersed after heartily cheering for the captain and his wife and child.

Captain Wolseley's unvarying thoughtfulness and consideration for those under his command seems to have gained him many friends, and his kindness is constantly very gratefully referred to in letters written to him at different times by officers who had formerly been midshipmen or lieutenants on board the different vessels he commanded. As one instance of his kindness, among many that might be mentioned:—One of the young midshipmen on the *San Josef*, when the fleet was in at Torbay, was extremely delicate; and long after that time, when the Admiral was quite an old man, and this officer had himself been for many years a post-captain, he came to see his old commander, whose kindness to him, he said, he should never forget; and turning to Admiral Wolseley's youngest daughter, who had never heard her father speak of the circumstance, or even mention the officer's name, he told her that when he was a little midshipman on board the *San Josef* he had a very severe and dangerous illness, and that her father had him removed from the ship to his house in Torquay, where he said he was so well nursed, and Captain and Mrs. Wolseley's kindness to him had been so great, that he fully believed the care they had taken of him had been the means of saving his life.

In the short memoir from which I have previously quoted, Admiral Wolseley mentions that "the fleet came into Torbay to await the signature of the Peace of Amiens, when," he adds, "we were paid off." This treaty was signed at Amiens early in the year 1802 ; but, as Captain Brenton remarks, "the preliminaries of peace were agreed on between the two great belligerents, France and England, late in the year 1801, although the definitive treaty was not signed till the following year."

Commenting upon this treaty, or rather truce, which lasted for little more than a year, he says : —"Buonaparte never intended more by the Peace of Amiens than to get home his troops and ships, dispersed in different parts of the world ; and having gained these points, he insulted Lord Whitworth, and seized our merchant-ships in the ports of France, under the most frivolous pretences ; in fact, he showed himself a man with whom an oath or a promise had no other meaning or object than to answer his own temporary purposes." However,

as Captain Brenton observes, "the peace, short and
bad as it was, gave us many advantages which we
should not otherwise have enjoyed."

Shortly after the crew of the *San Josef* were paid
off, Captain Wolseley was appointed to the command of the Sea Fencibles on the River Shannon.
According to Dr. Campbell, this corps was first
raised in England in the year 1798. "Early in
this year," he says, "Sir Home Popham proposed
a plan for the further protection and defence of
our coasts ; Sea Fencibles, composed of fishermen,
seamen employed in coasting-vessels, and all sea-
faring men engaged in the different harbours,
rivers, and creeks along the coast, were formed
into corps. These Fencibles were to be trained
to the use of the pike, and when they had an
opportunity, they were to be exercised with the
great guns. The whole coasts were divided into
districts, and over each district a post-captain and
a certain number of masters and commanders were
appointed. Protections were granted to all the Sea
Fencibles, which were to continue in force so long
as they regularly attended muster and exercise ;
besides this privilege, at each muster one shilling
was given to each man." Dr. Campbell then gives
a list of the English districts, the number of men
raised on those coasts which were supposed most
liable to invasion, &c. ; and adds :—" The Sea Fencibles were afterwards extended to other parts of
the kingdom." And some pages further on he

says that "orders were given early in the year 1801 for the construction of a great number of gunboats; these were stationed at the entrance of the principal ports and rivers in the kingdom, and the Sea Fencibles were instructed in their management."

Captain Wolseley held the appointment of captain of the Sea Fencibles in the River Shannon district till the year 1804. He was on the 23rd of April in that year advanced to the rank of Rear-Admiral, and was then placed in command of the Sea Fencibles all over Ireland.

On the 14th of August 1805, Admiral Wolseley's youngest son, Cosby William Wolseley, was born in Dublin, where the Admiral and Mrs. Wolseley were at that time living.[1] Shortly after the birth of his youngest son the Admiral gave up his appointment of commander of the Sea Fencibles in Ireland; and in the end of the year 1805, as he says in the little memoir from which I have hitherto quoted, he retired on his half-pay. It is a pity that so few details of his life and services in the navy have been given in the memoir, which ends abruptly at this point. The few further details concerning the subsequent years of Admiral Wolseley's life which I have been able to collect are taken chiefly from old letters and papers that have fortunately been preserved.

[1] Mr. Cosby Wolseley died, unmarried, on the 11th of March 1868.

On retiring from active service, Admiral Wolseley left Ireland and went to Bath, being probably induced to settle there by his uncle, Admiral Cosby, who had bought a house in that town and was then living there himself. Of the events of the next few years of Admiral Wolseley's life I find few records. Early in January 1808 Admiral Cosby died rather suddenly at his house in Bath, as appears from a letter to Admiral Wolseley written by Mr. Thomas Cosby, who had then succeeded, on his cousin's death, to the family estate of Stradbally Hall.

In the same year, 1808, on the 3rd of December, Admiral Wolseley's youngest daughter, Sydney Anne Wolseley, was born at Bath.[1] In 1810 Rear-Admiral Wolseley was promoted to the rank of Vice-Admiral "of the White Squadron of His Majesty's Fleet," as stated in the commission, which is dated the 31st of July 1810.

Two years later, apparently, from the following note written to him by the Earl of St. Vincent, Admiral Wolseley was trying to get some naval appointment or command; and although he does not seem to have succeeded in this, I give a copy of Lord St. Vincent's note, as, like the one from him previously quoted, it shows the high estimation in which Admiral Wolseley was held by

[1] Miss Sydney Wolseley married John Madden of Hilton Park, County Monaghan, J.P. and D.L., Colonel of the Monaghan Militia. Mrs. Madden survived her husband, and died in 1870.

the celebrated man under whom he had formerly
served :—

"DEAR SIR,—Nothing will give me, more real
satisfaction, than to bear Testimony, to your meritorious Conduct, when under my command, should
such proof be called for.

"Heartily wishing you success, in your present
pursuit, with every other blessing, to Mrs. Wolseley,
you, and Family, believe me to be very sincerely
yours,   ST. VINCENT.

"ROCHETTS, 11th Feby. 1812."

Next in date among the old papers still preserved appears an intimation issued from the
"Admiralty Office, 4th December 1813," that a
Commission had been signed by the "Lords Commissioners of the Admiralty," appointing Vice-
Admiral Wolseley (then of the White Squadron)
to the same rank in the Red Squadron, in consequence of "His Royal Highness the Prince
Regent having been pleased, in the name and on
the behalf of His Majesty, to order a Promotion of
Flag Officers of His Majesty's Fleet."

On the back of the paper Admiral Wolseley
wrote a copy of his reply, addressed to "John
Barrow, Esqre.," and dated "Teignmouth, Devon,
Decr. 8th, 1813." The Admiral ended his note to
that gentleman by saying :—"I beg you will be
pleased to acquaint their Lordships, that I am fully

sensible of the honour thus done me; and that I
am ready to serve whenever they may think proper
to employ me." From which it is evident that
the old Admiral would willingly have gone to sea
again if an appointment had been offered to him
at that time.

CHAPTER VII

DURING the period of Admiral Wolseley's residence in Bath he made frequent excursions to the seaside with Mrs. Wolseley and his children. Usually the summer was spent at some place on the coast of Devonshire, and at other times they went to the Continent for a few months. In the memorable year 1815 Admiral and Mrs. Wolseley and their two daughters were staying in Paris, just at the time when the Emperor Napoleon made his escape from the island of Elba.

The Emperor having landed at Cannes on the 1st of March, the news of this event soon arrived at Paris, and, of course, caused a great commotion among the English who were there at that time, but more particularly among English officers, both of the army and navy, who had at once to make hasty preparations for leaving Paris, for if they had remained they would most probably have been made prisoners of war, which would have been far from pleasant! Mr. John Ashton, author of a very interesting book entitled "Social England under the Regency," gives the following account of the sufferings of the English prisoners of war detained in France in the year 1811. Writing of events that occurred in England in the month of January in that year, he says :—" The French prisoners here were not treated too well, but the English prisoners in France were treated worse. Lloyd's was then the centre of benevolence, as the Mansion House now is, and the leading merchants and bankers issued an advertisement in the *Times* of January 7th, saying that their means of helping these prisoners were exhausted ; and they thus appealed for fresh funds :—

" ' The Committee beg to state that there are upwards of 10,000 British prisoners in the different prisons in France, for the most part in great distress, and that the subscription is intended for the alleviation of their sufferings in some degree, by assisting them with articles of clothing, bedding, fuel, and such other necessaries as they stand in most need of.' "

Mr. Ashton adds :—" Needless to say that the appeal was nobly responded to."   And he continues:—"Scant courtesy seems to have been paid to the prisoners on either side, almost degenerating into pettiness ; for this month an order was issued from Whitehall that no Frenchwomen should be allowed to land in this country who might have left France to see their husbands. The reason assigned for this very peculiar proceeding was, that the French Government would not permit Lady Lavie and family to join her husband, Sir Thomas, who was a prisoner at Verdun."

At the time Napoleon escaped from Elba, Sir
Thomas Lavie was living in Paris; and as he
was frequently a guest at the Tuileries, and had
many friends among the French royalist *noblesse*,
Admiral Wolseley, who was acquainted with him,
wrote to ask his opinion on the state of affairs,
and whether he thought they might safely remain
in Paris. In reply, Sir Thomas wrote the following little note, which he doubtless never imagined
would be handed down to posterity :—

"My dear Sir, — The accounts are greatly
exaggerated, and I see no occasion for alarm.
Nevertheless would recommend you to have your
passport in your pocket, and should the *army of
Elbe* advance to Lyons, you had better shove your
boat off.

" It has been publicly given out that the Duke
of Orleans has beaten the enemy and obliged him
to retire in confusion.—With best regards to you
and yours, I am, with a mutton chop on my fork,
ever yours,   T. L."

Notwithstanding the comforting intelligence publicly announced, rumours still continued afloat in
the town that, instead of retiring, Napoleon was
steadily continuing to advance, and that the regiments sent to oppose him had joined him instead.
When the truth of these rumours was positively
confirmed the excitement in Paris became still more

intense. Day after day in every street were to be seen carriages laden with luggage and crowded with people leaving the city.

At that time, when there were no railways, families who had not their own private carriages on the Continent usually travelled in small diligences hired for the journey. And the day before Admiral Wolseley and his family left Paris was one of no little anxiety for them all. The whole of the afternoon had been spent by the Admiral, who had been warned that there was no time to lose, in going from place to place where these carriages were to be hired, trying to engage one for their journey; but everywhere he went the proprietors had always the same answer to give — either all their carriages were already *en route* with refugees, or the few they had left were engaged. Feeling very tired, and much disheartened by his want of success, the Admiral was returning to his lodgings very late in the evening to get some dinner, when he fortunately met a friend, who said he had heard of another man who had a few carriages to let. This friend said he, too, was going home to dinner, and that immediately after it he would go to the place he had heard of for the Admiral, and would let him know the result that night.

A little after ten o'clock, to Admiral and Mrs. Wolseley's great relief, a message came from their friend to let them know he had been successful, and that the carriage would be at their door at a quarter to six in the morning, as the driver said they must not be later than that in starting. Miss Wolseley, who was then nearly fourteen years old, and her little sister, a child of eight, had been allowed to wait up for the expected message; they then went to their room with the intention of going to bed at once, but the scene in the street was so exciting that for a long time they could not make up their minds to leave the window.

The apartments occupied by Admiral Wolseley and his family were in a corner house, and consequently faced two streets; and during that night regiment after regiment, marching on their way to join Napoleon, with drums beating or bands playing—now a regiment of infantry, now one of cavalry, and occasionally a corps of artillery, with their heavy guns—passed the house in quick succession. The streets were crowded with people, who seemed to be in a wild state of excitement, some shouting, "*Vive le Roi!*" and others, "*Vive l'Empereur!*" as the troops passed; and many fights took place between the two parties, giving the gendarmes a great deal of trouble, trying to keep the peace between them.

At last, when there was a longer interval than usual, and no more troops were apparently coming, the two little girls went to bed, and being tired, soon fell asleep. But they were very shortly awakened, and much startled, by their maid, an Englishwoman, who rushed into their room, saying that they would "all be murdered if they remained in that dreadful place," and begging them to get up and dress at once, so as to be ready to "escape" the moment the carriage came. The immediate cause of her fearful state of alarm was, that a more desperate battle than any that had yet taken place was then going on between the Imperialists and Royalists, just under the windows. The fight was raging furiously when Miss Wolseley and her sister looked out. The scene in the street and the shouts and cries were dreadful; and when the gendarmes at last succeeded in dispersing the combatants, the two girls were too much excited to think of going back to bed, and they therefore took the maid's advice, and dressed as quickly as they could.

Although the disturbance was ended and the streets were almost deserted by the time the carriage came, the little family party were no doubt very glad to leave Paris, and probably felt much more at their ease when the towers of Notre Dame had vanished in the distance!

At Bruges, where Admiral Wolseley and his family arrived about eleven o'clock at night, people seemed to be in almost as excited a state as those they had left in Paris. Late as the hour was when they arrived, in every street their carriage passed through, crowds of people were to be seen walking about or standing in groups before the doors, just as if it had been the middle of the day. The Admiral had taken the precaution of writing to engage rooms at the best hotel; and as all the party were tired after their long journey, they went to bed as soon as they could do so.

The house, however, was crowded with refugees from Paris, and the noise was so great, caused by the constant running up and down stairs and talking in the passages, that Miss Wolseley, tired as she was, could not get to sleep for some time. At last the inmates appeared to be getting more quiet, and she was just dozing off, when she was roused by the sound of a horse clattering, apparently at full gallop, over the pavement into the court-yard, after which the noise and commotion in the hotel became worse than ever. A few minutes later the landlady knocked at all their doors, and begged them to get up at once; she said she had reserved her best apartments for the Admiral and his family, but that she must now ask them to give them up, as a courier had just arrived to engage rooms for King Louis XVIII. of France. She said that the man had told her that the King had a large party of gentlemen with him, and that there were three or four carriages full of people, who would be there in about twenty minutes.

Finding that there was not even a garret un-occupied in the house, Admiral Wolseley went out to try to get rooms at some of the other hotels; and Mrs. Wolseley and her daughters got up and dressed as quickly as they could. Before they had quite finished, the King and his party arrived, and the landlady again came up to beg that they would leave the rooms as soon as possible, so as to allow them to be prepared for his Majesty. Accordingly, the moment they were dressed they went down to the hall, which they found crowded with people, among whom were a number of Belgian and French officers. One of the latter came forward very politely to Mrs. Wolseley and expressed his regret at the inconvenience they had been put to in having to give up their rooms. He afterwards asked Miss Wolseley if she would like to see the King, and offering his arm, he took her down a passage to an open door at which a crowd of people were standing looking in. They instantly made way for her, and she had a good opportunity of seeing his Majesty, who was engaged in eating his supper, and was sitting at the other side of a long table, exactly facing the door at which she and the officer were standing.

During the exile of the French royal family in England, some members of the house of Bourbon had paid a visit to Bath, but although Miss Wolseley had seen the King's brother, afterwards Charles X., and the Duchesse d'Angoulême, the princess of whom Napoleon had said that she was "the only *man* of the family," it so happened that she had never before seen Louis XVIII. himself.

There were a number of gentlemen sitting at

L

the table with the King, and the officer who was with Miss Wolseley, and who had probably come from Paris with the party, appeared to know them all, and told her who every one was. There were probably other people of note present, but she only afterwards remembered the names of Field-Marshals MacDonald and Berthier. Both were generals who had distinguished themselves in Napoleon's campaigns, and had been raised to the peerage by the Emperor. Berthier, who had been created Prince of Neuchâtel and Wagram, had in 1810 acted as Napoleon's proxy at the marriage of Marie Louise at Vienna. Miss Wolseley thought Marshal MacDonald a very handsome man, and she looked at him with much interest, being aware that he was descended from a Scotch gentleman who had fought for Prince Charles Edward, "the young Chevalier."

Shortly after she had returned to the hall, where she had left her mother and sister, the Admiral came in. He said no rooms were to be had in any of the hotels, as they were all crowded. It was then nearly three o'clock A.M., and at that hour it would, of course, have been useless to attempt to look for lodgings; so he said he had engaged a carriage, which would be there directly, to take them on to Ghent.

They remained in that ancient city for some time. King Louis arrived there a few days after them, and Admiral Wolseley, having heard that most of the English officers then in the town were calling to pay their respects to his Majesty, went one day to the hotel where the King was staying. He was shown upstairs to a sitting-room, where he found a number of gentlemen, one of whom, Marshal MacDonald, came forward and took his card to the King, and returning in a few minutes, he conducted Admiral Wolseley into the presence of his Majesty, who, I believe, received him very graciously.

Being utterly ignorant, however, of what passed during Admiral Wolseley's interview with King Louis XVIII., I can give no account of their conversation. And by way of compensating the reader for the loss of what might have been a narrative of absorbing interest, I beg leave to offer the following extract from a little book entitled "Narrative of a Residence in Belgium during the Campaign of 1815," by "An Englishwoman."

This lady, who, it appears, arrived at Ghent from Bruges on the evening of Tuesday the 13th of June, spent the following day in sight-seeing, and probably considered it advisable not to miss such a good opportunity of seeing King Louis XVIII. of France, of whom, however, she does not give a very flattering description. She says :—

"The city of Ghent seemed to be restored to some traces of its ancient grandeur by the temporary residence of the Bourbon princes and the little expatriated Court of Louis XVIII. I had never been able to feel any extravagant degree of attachment to this unfortunate royal family; their restoration had not given me any enthusiastic joy, nor their fall much sorrow; and even the honour of paying my *devoirs* to Louis le Désiré, and exchanging some profound and reverential bows and courtesies with His Most Catholic Majesty, failed to inspire me with much interest or admiration for this persecuted princely race. These bows, by the way, cost the good old King considerable time and labour, for he is extremely unwieldy and corpulent and gouty, and he looks very lethargic and snuffy; and it is really a thousand pities that an exiled and dethroned monarch should be so remarkably uninteresting a personage."

From Ghent Admiral Wolseley and his family went to Ostend, where they spent a few weeks; and when they wished to leave that port, shortly before the battle of Waterloo, they found it no easy matter to do so, all the regular passenger-packets having been engaged by the Government for the transport of troops. After a delay of some days, and being anxious to return home, they engaged berths in a trading-ship bound for Dover. A number of other people, both English and foreign, took the same opportunity of crossing, and the vessel, which was by no means a large one, was crowded with passengers—there being fifty-four in all. Among the number there was an officer of the distinguished regiment known

as the "Black Brunswickers," who was going to
London with despatches.

Just before the vessel left the quay at Ostend,
one of the passenger-packets, with the 42nd High-
landers on board, came in at the other side of
the ship, and in order to land, the whole regiment crossed the deck, upon which Admiral
Wolseley and his family were standing. A
number of the soldiers, in their hurry to land,
jumped on board the ship from the packet in
which they had arrived. This regiment suffered
dreadfully at Waterloo, and many of those brave
men who that day, full of life and vigour, landed
at Ostend lost their lives very shortly afterwards
in that terrible battle.

After the ship had sailed from Ostend it passed,
at a distance, no less than fourteen transports
crowded with British troops making their way
into that port. The wind was blowing freshly
then, and Admiral Wolseley and his family had
a very rough passage; and when they were a
little more than half-way across, a terrible storm
came on in the course of the night. The ship
was an old one, and, with a heavy cargo on
board, it was very low in the water, and was
for some hours in great danger of being lost.
In the middle of the night the captain went
down and roused Admiral Wolseley, who was
fast asleep in the cabin, and asked him to come
to his assistance. The Admiral at once went

on deck, and as he considered that it would
be dangerous under the circumstances to try to
make Dover, the port for which they were bound,
he proposed that they should bring the vessel
in at Lowestoft instead. The captain agreed to
this, and gave up the command of the ship to
Admiral Wolseley, who, of course, was perfectly
acquainted with the navigation of every part of
the Channel. The Admiral remained on deck
for the rest of the night, and brought the vessel
in quite safely at Lowestoft early next day.
Many of the passengers were extremely grateful
to him for his exertions during the night, and
before going on shore thanked him most warmly
for having, as they said, "saved their lives."

CHAPTER VIII

WITHIN the short space of one month after Admiral Wolseley returned to England, events of the greatest importance had followed each other in quick succession. The battle of Waterloo had been fought and won by our gallant army, and in less than a month after that glorious 18th of June, when "les grandes lignes rouges" had stood their ground so bravely, as Messieurs Erckmann and Chatrian describe them, "immobiles dans la fumée comme des murs," the extraordinary man whose insatiable ambition had caused so much bloodshed and misery in Europe was virtually a prisoner on board the British man-of-war *Bellerophon.*

The author of "Social England under the Regency," a book from which I have already given an extract, says :—"On the 15th of July 1815 Napoleon and suite went on board the *Bellerophon,*" where, as the writer remarks, "he was treated with every consideration by Captain Maitland. He was still looked upon as Emperor, and dined off his own gold plate, the dinner being ordered by his own *maître d'hôtel,* and

when he visited the *Superb* he was received with
all the honour awarded to royalty, with the exception of a salute being fired."

Among Admiral Wolseley's papers are two
very interesting letters written by his eldest son,
Mr. John Wolseley, in which a description is
given of the Emperor's visit to the last-mentioned ship. The young writer apparently entered
the navy in 1814, or shortly before that year,
as Lord St. Vincent says in a note to Admiral
Wolseley, written from his country place, Rochetts,
and dated "13th May 1814":—"I heartily hope
Mrs. Wolseley, you, and the young folk enjoy
good health, and that the young sailor is going
on well."

In the following year, 1815, when the Emperor
Napoleon, as one of the midshipmen on board the
Bellerophon writes, "in an evil hour, formed the
resolution of placing himself under the protection of the British flag," Mr. John Wolseley was
serving as a midshipman on board Admiral Sir
Henry Hotham's flag-ship, the *Superb*. And before
giving copies of his two letters, I now proceed to
take some passages, which I think will add to
their interest, from the "Reminiscences of Napoleon," written by the young officer of the
Bellerophon previously referred to,[1] who says:—
"After two interviews with the Duke of Rovigo,

---

[1] These "Reminiscences of Napoleon" are given in an auto-
biography published in 1838 "by a Midshipman of the *Bellerophon*."

Las Casas, and Captain Maitland, it was finally agreed that the Emperor should come on board the *Bellerophon* on the morning of the 15th of July."

"The evening of the 14th was calm and delightful," the writer continues, "as we lay at single anchor in Basque roads awaiting the great event of the morrow. . . . I had the middle watch, and just as I was relieved, about half-past four in the morning of the 15th—and a lovely morning it was—we saw a man-of-war brig get under weigh from Aix roads and stand out towards us, bearing a flag of truce. The wind, however, was blowing direct in her teeth, so that she made little of it, and it became evident that it would be several hours before she reached us. While the other midshipmen of the watch slipped off to their hammocks to have a snooze before breakfast, I could not think of sleep, but stood anxiously watching the short tacks of *L'Épervier*, which now 'carried Cæsar and his fortunes.'

"About six in the morning the look-out man at the mast-head announced a large ship of war standing direct in for the roadstead, which Captain Maitland suspecting to be the *Superb*, bearing the flag of Admiral Sir Henry Hotham, he gave immediate orders to hoist out the barge, and despatched her, under the command of the first lieutenant, to the French brig, being apprehensive that, if the admiral arrived before the brig got out, Napoleon would deliver himself up to the admiral instead of to us, and thus have lost us so much honour.

"As our barge approached the brig hove to, and from the moment she came alongside we watched every motion with deep anxiety. Like all Napoleon's movements, he was not slow even in this, his last free act. The barge had not remained ten minutes alongside before we saw the rigging of the brig crowded with men, persons stepping down the side into the boat, and the next moment she shoved off and gave way for the ship, while the waving of the men's hats in the rigging and the cheering which we heard faintly in the distance left no doubt that the expected guest was approaching. A general's guard of marines was ordered aft on the quarter-deck, and the boatswain stood, whistle in hand, ready to do the honours of the side. The lieu-tenants stood grouped first on the quarter-deck, and we more humble middies behind them, while the captain, evidently in much anxiety, kept trudging backwards and forwards between the gangway and his own cabin, sometimes peeping out at one of the quarter-deck ports to see if the barge was drawing near.

"It is a sin," the writer continues, "to mix up any trifling story with so great an event; but a circumstance occurred so laughable of itself, rendered more so from the solemnity of the occasion, that I cannot resist mentioning it. While in this state of eager expectation, a young midshipman, one of the Bruces of Kennet, I think, walked very demurely up to Manning, the boatswain, who was standing all importance at the gangway, and after comically eyeing his squat figure and bronzed countenance, Bruce gently laid hold of one of his whiskers, to which the boatswain good naturedly submitted, as the youngster was a great favourite with him.

"'Manning,' says he, most sentimentally, 'this is the proudest day of your life ; you are this day to do the honours of the side to the greatest man the world ever produced, or ever will produce.'

"Here the boatswain eyed him with proud delight.

"'And along with the great Napoleon, the name of Manning, the boatswain of the *Bellerophon*, will go down to the latest posterity ; and, as a relic of that great man, permit me, my dear Manning, to preserve a lock of your hair.'

"Here he made an infernal tug at the boatswain's immense whisker, and fairly carried away a part of it, making his way through the crowd and down below with the speed of an arrow. The infuriated boatswain, finding he had passed so rapidly from the sublime to the ridiculous, through the instrumentality of this imp of a youngster, could vent his rage in no other way but by making his

glazed hat spin full force after his tantaliser with"
[an oath which I take the liberty of omitting].
"The hat, however, fell far short of young Bruce,
and the noise and half burst of laughter the trick
occasioned drew the attention of the captain, who,
coming up, with a 'What, what's all this? the poor
boatswain was glad to draw to his hat and resume
his position.

"The barge approached, and ranged alongside.
The first lieutenant came up the side, and to Maitland's eager and blunt question, 'Have you got
him?' he answered in the affirmative. After the
lieutenant came Savary, followed by Marshal Bertrand, who bowed and fell back a pace on the
gangway to await the ascent of their master. And
now came the little, great man himself, wrapped
up in his grey greatcoat buttoned to the chin,
three-cocked hat and Hussar boots, without any
sword, I suppose as emblematical of his changed
condition. Maitland received him with every mark
of respect, as far as look and deportment could
indicate, but he was *not* received with the respect
due to a crowned head. So far from that, the
captain, on Napoleon's addressing him, only removed his hat, as to a general officer, and remained
covered while the Emperor spoke to him. His
expressions were brief, I believe only reiterating
what he had stated the day previous in his letter
to the Prince Regent, 'that he placed himself
under the protection of the British nation, and

under that of the British commander as the repre-
sentative of his sovereign.' The captain again
moved his hat, and turned to conduct the Emperor
to the cabin. As he passed through the officers
assembled on the quarter-deck he repeatedly bowed
slightly to us and smiled.

"We were engaged during the forenoon of the
15th bringing on board the suite and luggage of
the Emperor from *L'Épervier* brig. About ten
o'clock Napoleon appeared on deck, . . . in the
dress now known to all the world; but he had
exchanged his long boots for silk stockings, shoes,
and gold buckles. . . . The sun shone as bright on
the fallen Emperor as it did on the glorious morning of Austerlitz. The fine figure of Madame Bertrand,[1] with her charming children, adorned our
quarter-deck. A great many officers in rich uniforms came off with Napoleon, who did not eventually follow him to St. Helena.[2] These were all
grouped about this fine morning, making the deck
of the old ship (which was scrubbed and washed
to the bones) look as gay as a drawing-room on
a *levée* day. Maitland, quite in his element, kept
jogging about with his slight stoop and Scotch burr,

---

[1] The young midshipman invariably calls Madame Bertrand "Lady
Bertrand" in writing about her, and I have taken the liberty of
altering this.

[2] In an article in the *Times* of July 25, 1815, quoted by Mr.
Ashton, it is stated that "Buonaparte's suite, as it is called, consists
of upwards of forty persons, among whom are Bertrand, Savary,
L'Allemand," &c., &c.; and the midshipman mentions also Las
Casas, Montholon, and Mesdames Bertrand and Montholon.

sometimes acting the gallant to Madame Bertrand, and then, all attention, listening to and answering the many questions put to him by the Emperor. He expressed a wish to go through the ship; the captain took the lead, the Emperor followed, and his little *cortège* of marshals in full uniform brought up the rear. . . . He made the round of both decks, complimented Maitland on the excellent order of the ship—which was no flattery, for she was in capital fighting condition—asked questions of any of the men who came in his way, and a young middy who, boy-like, had got before the Emperor, and was gazing up in his face, he honoured with a tap on the head and a pinch by the ear, and, smiling, put him to a side, which the youngster declared was the highest honour he had ever received in his life, viz., to have his ears pinched by the great Napoleon !!!

"Returning to the quarter-deck, he expressed a wish to speak to the boatswain, to put some questions to him relative to his duty, there being a considerable difference in the responsibility of that officer in the French service, I understand, from that on board our ships. The boatswain was sent for, and upon Maitland telling him the Emperor wished to speak with him, the boatswain shuffled up to Napoleon, and pulling off his narrow-brimmed glazed scraper, made a duck with his head, accompanied by a scrape of the right foot. 'I hope,' says he, 'I see your honour well.' Napoleon, who did not understand as much English, asked Captain Maitland what he said, which I have no doubt the captain translated faithfully, for he was blunt enough in his own way. The Emperor smiled, and proceeded to put his questions to the boatswain through the medium of the captain ; and as Napoleon seemed quite well pleased when he dismissed him, I have no doubt the rough old fellow had answered much to the purpose, for although he did not understand court manners, he perfectly understood his duty.

" About twelve the *Superb* entered the roadstead, and the moment she came to an anchor Admiral Hotham came on board, and was introduced to the Emperor on the quarter-deck. Sir Henry immediately uncovered, and remained so while he was on board. This was the signal for that which, I believe, every one of us desired. The captain followed the example of the admiral, and in future every one uncovered while the Emperor was on deck, thus treating him with the respect due to a crowned head."

The writer says Napoleon "was evidently pleased with the deportment of Hotham and Maitland, looked quite at ease, and as completely at home as if he had been going a pleasure-trip on board of one of his own imperial yachts." He then adds :—" The first day passed away most delightfully ; the captain slung his cot in the wardroom and relinquished his cabin to the Emperor, henceforth becoming only his guest." Upon which proceeding he makes the following somewhat amusing comment :—"This was noble and generous, and nothing further need be mentioned of Maitland to show that he had an excellent heart."

Although the *Bellerophon* was a ship of seventy-four guns, it was very probably rather difficult to find accommodation for so many people in addition to the crew, but doubtless the honour of taking the Emperor to England fully compensated for any inconvenience they suffered. And the next morning, the 16th of July, when Napoleon was going to pay his visit on board the *Superb*, the midshipman says "so much alarmed was the ship's company lest he might not be allowed to return to the *Bellerophon* that they came aft in a body to Captain Maitland to state their intention of resisting by force any attempt of Admiral Hotham to obtain the person of Napoleon, and were only satisfied when Maitland assured them that no such thing was intended."

The following account of what afterwards took place on the morning of the 16th is given by the same writer :—"The Emperor," he says, "accompanied by Captain Maitland, went on board the *Superb* to breakfast with Sir Henry Hotham, according to the invitation of the previous day. Before the Emperor left the ship the whole body

of our marines were drawn up on the quarter-
deck to receive him with all due honour as he
came out of the cabin. As he passed the
marines and returned their military salute of
arms, ever fond of warlike display, he suddenly
stopped, his eye brightened, and crossing the
deck, he minutely examined the arms and
accoutrements of the marines—and a fine body of
men they were—requested the captain of marines
(Marshall) to put the men through one or two
movements, and when they had performed these,
he pointed to him to bring them to the charge.
In our army the front rank only charges, but,
I believe, in the French the second rank keeps
poking over the shoulders of the first—as likely
to kill their own men as the enemy. Napoleon
put aside the bayonet of one of our front-rank
men, and taking hold of the musket of the
second-rank man, made a sign to him to point his
musket between the two front-rank men, asking
Captain Marshall at the same time if he did not
think that mode of charge preferable to ours.
To which the captain replied that it might be so,
but it was generally allowed that our mode of
charge had been *very effectual.* Here the Emperor
took a most conscious look at the captain of
marines, as much as to say, 'I know that, to
my cost,' and, smiling, turned to Bertrand, to whom
he observed, 'How much might be done with two
hundred thousand such fine fellows as these!'"

M

In these extracts I have given the whole of the midshipman's description of the Emperor Napoleon's reception on board the *Bellerophon*, and the account of the principal incidents of his first day in that vessel. And having brought this little history to the morning of the 16th, when he went to breakfast with Admiral Sir Henry Hotham in the *Superb*, I may now give a copy of the first of Mr. John Wolseley's letters, in which will be found a description of the visit.

Before I copy the letter I should, however, mention that Captain Grace, R.N.,[1] the gentleman to whom it was written, was an old friend of Admiral Wolseley, to whom he very kindly sent that and another letter he had received from Mr. John Wolseley, in which many little details are given which are not noted by the midshipman of the *Bellerophon*, and these two interesting letters therefore supply some missing links in his narrative.

However, to return to the visit of "the little, great man" on board of the *Superb*. The midshipman of the *Bellerophon* says :—"The moment our barge left the ship, the *Superb's* yards were manned with the pick of her ship's company, dressed in their blue jackets and white duck

---

[1] Captain Grace was in the year 1815 acting as private secretary to the Marquis of Buckingham, afterwards first Duke of Buckingham, who, *I think*, was at that time First Lord of the Admiralty.

trousers, and her complement of marines drawn up on the quarter-deck to receive the wonderful stranger." Of his visit the midshipman merely remarks that "his reception by the admiral was everything that he could wish, and he remained nearly two hours on board the *Superb*." And Mr. John Wolseley writes the following account :—

"'H.M.S. SUPERB,'
BASQUE ROADS, *July* 20, 1815.

"My dear Captain Grace, — We have been going on very quietly here, supplying the Royalists with arms, without anything taking place to interrupt the regular routine till Saturday last when we came in here and found Buonaparte on board the *Bellerophon*. As it will probably interest you I shall tell all that happened on the occasion. He had just left the French brig that brought him from Isle D'Aix with his suite, consisting of Savary, Duke of Rovigo, Counts Bertrand, Las Casas, Montholon, etc. etc. Mesdames Bertrand and Montholon had also come with him. He immediately took possession of Captain Maitland's cabin, got all his own plate &c. into it, and sent to ask Captn. M. to Breakfast with him. On Sunday he came on board of us to a *dejeuné* at 10 o'clock; we manned yards for him and received him with every demonstration of respect and honour. He then went round the ship and looked at every-

thing. Nothing appeared to escape him. We
were all presented to him by his own request.
He is very short and very fat, and was consequently much tired with walking up and down
the ladders. There was nothing in the appearance of this extraordinary man that I thought
particularly striking; he was very like the prints
I had seen of him. His likeness is preserved
throughout in a Burlesque called Dr. Syntax's
life of Buonaparte which you may perhaps have
seen. The print of the Battle of Leipsic page
233 shows him flying on horseback as correctly
in shape and feature (allowing a little for the
exaggeration of caricatures) as it is possible to
be. He appeared extremely affable and asked
a great many questions; once he enquired of
the Admiral if we were not rather disappointed
in the American war. It struck me he was in
full possession of that talent so much esteemed
by soldiers, called the military *coup d'œil* (I
believe), for a rapid glance at the objects
around him appeared to satisfy him fully as to
their condition and position. He was plain in
his dress, and did not seem depressed in spirits
by his misfortunes. It will no doubt be matter
of great exultation in England, when they find
the conqueror of the continent in their possession.
I am anxious to know what they mean to do
with him. His *Captivity* by the bye will put an
end to all your hopes of employment, as it has

to my hopes of promotion. I think I shall just serve my time out to be ready for another war, and leave the service. I sincerely hope however that this peace may prove a lasting one (when it comes). But my letter will be late if I do not conclude so believe me to remain yours truly,

" J. H. WOLSELEY."

The midshipman of the *Bellerophon*, to whose " Reminiscences " I now return, says :—" While our barge was lying alongside the *Superb*, waiting for the Emperor and Captain Maitland, a conversation took place between some of the *Superb's* men and our boat's crew, in which the former insisted that *they*, and not us, were to have the honour of carrying Napoleon to England, while our men stood stoutly out for their prerogative, as being the first who received him on board. ' No, no,' says one of the *Superb's*, ' depend upon it the admiral will take Boney home himself, and will not allow you to have anything more to do with him.' ' Will he ? ' answers one of the *Bellerophon's*, with an oath. ' Before we suffer that, my boy, we shall give you *ten* rounds and secure first.' Ten rounds and secure," the midshipman explains, " had become a by-word in the ship, as for some weeks previous to Napoleon's coming on board we had been kept close at quarters exercising the guns, and to go through the motions of ' ten rounds and secure ' had been the common spell at quarters, so that

our man thought we would try the effect of our
ten rounds upon the *Superb*, sooner than quit
Boney."

However, all anxiety of the crew of the *Bellerophon* upon that point was speedily at an end.
And the midshipman says :—"The Emperor returned from the *Superb* about 2 P.M., when we
immediately weighed, and made all sail for England." And he continues :— "I remarked little
more of him that day, but on the morning of the
17th he was early on the quarter-deck, putting
questions in broken English, almost unintelligible,
to all who crossed his path."

The midshipman says little about the voyage
to England, and apparently was only personally
addressed on two occasions by the Emperor ; and
as he does not seem to have thought of collecting
any anecdotes about him from others, as Mr. John
Wolseley did, he has consequently little that is
interesting to relate.

Of the first time Napoleon spoke to him he
remarks :—"The Emperor seemed to entertain an
idea that the Americans were bigger men than us,
for whenever he saw any very stout man he asked
him if he was an American." And he adds :—"I
happened to be blessed with a tolerable length of
limb, and as I was pacing the lee side of the
quarter-deck, along with a big raw-boned Irishman,
a brother-in-law of Captain Maitland's, Napoleon
stepped over to us, putting his usual question,

'How long have you been in the service? Of what country?' And without allowing any time for reply, he turned round and asked Maitland 'if we were not Americans?'"

The next time the Emperor addressed him was, as he says, the "morning we made Ushant." And he continues :—"I had come on deck at four in the morning to take the morning watch, and the washing of the decks had just begun, when, to my astonishment, I saw the Emperor come out of the cabin at that early hour and make for the poop-ladder. From the wetness of the decks, he was in danger of falling at every step, and I immediately stepped up to him, hat in hand, and tendered him my arm, which he laid hold of at once, smiling, and pointing to the poop, saying in broken English, 'The poop, the poop'; he ascended the poop-ladder leaning on my arm, and having gained the deck, he quitted his hold and mounted upon a gun-slide, nodding and smiling thanks for my attention, and pointing to the land, he said, 'Ushant, Cape Ushant?' I replied, 'Yes, sire,' and withdrew. He then took out a pocket-glass, and applied it to his eye, looking eagerly at the land. In this position he remained from five in the morning to nearly midday, without paying any attention to what was passing around him, or speaking to one of his suite, who had been standing behind him for several hours. No wonder he thus gazed; it was the last look at the land of his glory, and I am convinced he felt it such."

The same writer says :—"Amongst other plans for killing the time, and lightening the tedium of a sea-passage to the refugees, we bethought us of getting up a play. This was managed by one of the lieutenants of marines, a fellow of great taste, and some one or two of the midshipmen who pre-tended to skill in the Shakespearian art. What the piece was I do not recollect, but when it was an-nounced to the Emperor by Captain Maitland, and the immortal honour of his imperial presence begged for a few minutes, he laughed very heartily, consented instantly, and turning to Madame Ber-trand, told her that she must stand his interpreter. The stage was fitted up between decks, more, I am afraid, in ship-shape than theatrical style ; and, sure enough, Napoleon and his whole suite attended. He was much amused with those who took the female parts ; . . . and after good-naturedly sitting for nearly twenty minutes, he rose, smiled to the actors, and retired.

"We had fine weather," the writer continues, "during the few days we were at sea before we made the English coast, and, seemingly regardless of the future, the daily turn-out on the quarter-deck was quite gay and reviving. We were always sure of a sight of the Emperor and the chief part of his suite immediately after dinner, when he generally remained on deck for about half-an-hour. Madame

Bertrand, Captain Maitland, Bertrand, Savary, L'Allemande, Las Casas, and his aide-de-camp, Montholon, formed the principal figures of the group ranged round the Emperor, while we young gentlemen took up our station on the poop, to feast our eyes with a sight of the great man. . . . He generally kept his gold snuff-box in his hand while in conversation." And the writer adds :—"Notwithstanding that we have him invariably drawn and" —as he rather oddly expresses it—"busted with his arms folded across his breast, I never saw him in that attitude but once during the whole three weeks we had him on board."

Of the conversations in which the great man took part during these walks upon the deck, the writer from whom I have been quoting could evidently give no account. And Mr. John Wolseley in his second letter gives many interesting particulars, which he heard afterwards from the second lieutenant of his own ship, who had been sent home with despatches in the *Bellerophon* by Sir Henry Hotham. Mr. Wolseley's letter has unfortunately been slightly torn, and, as the reader will remark, I have tried to replace some missing words :—

"*Sept.* 12, 1815.
NORFOLK CRESCENT, BATH.

"MY DEAR CAPTAIN GRACE,—I have no farther excuse to offer for delaying to answer your kind letter, but the hurry and confusion of being paid

off, and the anxiety I suffered whilst endeavouring to obtain leave of absence, which as you will perceive from the date of this, I have been so fortunate as to procure. I remain at home for a month at least, in which time I am in hopes that parental care will again re-establish my health and render me strong enough to get through the winter. I had an attack of my breath complaint on the coast of France, which has weakened me a good deal, though it has now, thank God, entirely left me. We were paid off on the 6th inst., and I am re-entered again on *Superb's* Books by the friendly care of Sir H. Hotham who recommended me to Captain Ekins. I am afraid your kindness has made you over-rate my attempt at a description of Buonaparte; and I am afraid Lady Buckingham will not find so much amusement in my account as you seem to hope. However, believe me, it gives me great pleasure to think that I have afforded any gratification to yourself or friend. I have, according to your wishes, endeavoured to collect what anecdotes I could of this extraordinary man; but you most likely will not find much that you do not already know. I am not aware of Sir H. H.'s. opinion about his going to St. Helena, but I know he is very much vexed at the animadversions made upon his conduct. I rejoice that he has a friend in the Highlands of [Scotland[1]] who

[1] On the outside of the letter there is the following memorandum, most probably written by Captain Grace :—"Recd. Sept. 28th, 1815, Keith Hall, Aberdeenshire."

can so ably defend his [conduct?] if necessary.
I believe I told you Nap always makes use of
an opera glass, and has such insinuating manners,
and such an air that while looking at him you
cannot help feeling something of admiration and
respect which makes you forget his former crimes.
I can call it nothing but a species of fascination,
if I may be allowed the expression for a man. He
could not talk English, but soon found out such
of the foremast men in the *Bellerophon* that could
talk French, and talked to them about the actions
they had been in, and their country, &c., with so
much affability that they were completely charmed.
I think it appears to be his *forte* to act with the
greatest courtesy without ever overstepping the
dignity of an Emperor, so that everything he does
seems the condescension of a great man. He frequently converses with Madame Bertrand (who is
a charming woman, as to her manners, I mean,
and through whom he circulates what he wishes
to be known) upon the subject of the Battle of
Waterloo, and says it was the hardest contested
one he ever fought. He pays high compliments
to our infantry, and to the Scotch Greys, though
he thinks his cavalry upon the whole superior to
ours. He acknowledges that if Lord Paget had
not been wounded, he would in two minutes have
had his hand upon him. He says had he had
English infantry he would have gained the day.
He wishes to make out that he had only 55,000

men *actually* engaged, of which number he lost
25,000. If Grouché had occupied the ground he
ordered we were to have lost the Battle. He made
many observations to Captn. Maitland of the difference between the French and English ships, and
observed that he could not get such men; he said
something to the same effect about the army, and
allows that Englishmen stand *beating better* than
Frenchmen. He allows that Lord Wellington is
equally as good a general as himself, and has more
prudence. This is interesting, because you may
recollect that story of some one telling him (at
Elba, I believe) that 'Lord W. was the best in
the world';—to which he replied, 'We have never
met.' On the 19th July he related the cause
of his quarrel with Sir S. Smith. Sir S. Smith
issued a proclamation (he says) inviting his soldiers
to desert;—he in return declared him *mad*, and
interdicted all communication with him. Sir S. then
sent him a challenge, which he said he would accept
when the Duke of Marlborough or some such great
men came out; (meaning that Sir S. was not of
sufficient consequence). He compares himself to
Themistocles;—he says, if Mr. Fox had lived, [he,
himself?] should not now have been where he is,
and that he should have had the order of the garter.
Speaking of the sea, he says, 'it is a horrible element, but there is no keeping you English off it;
if it had not been for you, I should have been
Emperor of the earth.' He speaks highly of the

Superb and the treatment he received in her; he asked who the purser was, and upon being told he was 'un commissaire,' he asked if he was not a great rogue. He thought the *Cusacoa*, which he had seen off Elba, too fine to be a fighting ship— but, added Madame Bertrand, 'you English have so many ships for fighting, I suppose you can spare something for show.' I believe you may rely on the correctness of this statement, as I had it from Mr. Fletcher our 2nd Lieut. who went in the *Bellerophon* with the despatches. We are all very well here, and my father and mother join with me in best wishes and remembrances to you. I hope you will be able to read this long scrawl, the subject has betrayed me into prolixity.—Yours truly,   J. H. WOLSELEY.'

The great interest that is still, apparently, felt in everything connected with the celebrated man, of whom so good a description has been given by the two young midshipmen, tempts me to take the following extract from Mr. Ashton's "Social England under the Regency," in which will be found an amusing account of the excitement there was in England about him when the *Bellerophon* arrived.

"On the 16th of July," writes Mr. Ashton, "they set sail for England, and at daybreak on the 24th they were close to Dartmouth. Napoleon rose at six, and went on the poop, surveying the coast, which he much admired, exclaiming, 'What a

beautiful country! It very much resembles Porto
Ferrajo at Elba.'" On the same day they anchored
at Torbay, "and no sooner was it known," writes
Mr. Ashton, "that Napoleon was on board the
Bellerophon than the bay was covered with vessels
and boats full of people.

"On July 26th orders came for the *Bellerophon*
to go to Plymouth, which being reached, two
frigates, the *Liffey* and *Eurotas*, were anchored, one
at either side of her, and kept strict guard over her.
Visitors from London and all parts of England
came to get a glimpse of him, and the sea was
literally alive with boats of every description." Mr.
Ashton then gives some extracts from a contem-
porary pamphlet :—"Napoleon generally walked
the quarter-deck about eleven in the forenoon, and
about five in the afternoon. He ate but two meals
in the day, both alike ; meat of every description,
different wines, coffee, fruit, &c. Immediately after
each meal, he rose first, and the others followed ;
he then went on the quarter-deck, or in the after-
cabin to study.

"Upwards of one thousand boats were from
morning to night round the *Bellerophon*. The
seamen of the *Bellerophon* adopted a curious mode
to give an account to the spectators in the boats of
the movements of Napoleon. They wrote in chalk
on a board, which they exhibited, a short account
of his different occupations : 'At breakfast'; 'In
the cabin with Captain Maitland'; 'Writing with

his officers'; 'Going to dinner'; 'Coming upon deck'; &c."

Mr. Ashton continues:—"Las Casas says: 'It was known that he always appeared on deck towards five o'clock. A short time before this hour all the boats collected alongside of each other; there were thousands, and so closely were they connected that the water could no longer be seen between them.'"

The midshipman of the *Bellerophon*, too, says:— "The sound was literally covered with boats; the weather was delightful; the ladies looked as gay as butterflies; bands of music in several of the boats played favourite French airs, to attract, if possible, the Emperor's attention, that they might get a sight of him"; and he remarks that Napoleon "showed no disinclination to gratify the eager spectators by frequently appearing at the gangway, examining the crowd with his pocket-glass," and often bowing and smiling "with evident satisfaction."

"During the few days we lay at Plymouth Sound," the writer continues, "some very disagreeable circumstances, and even some accidents, occurred, in consequence of a parcel of heavy boats from the dockyard having been sent off to row guard round the ship, to keep off the spectators. This duty was performed with great rudeness, and when the rush of boats took place, when Napoleon appeared at the gangway, coming in violent contact with those heavy dockyard boats, which kept rowing at full speed round the ship, the screams of the ladies and the oaths of the men seemed to give Napoleon great annoyance.

" The signal for the Emperor's being on deck was the officers uncovering.   No sooner was this ceremony noticed than the rush from without took place, and the screaming and swearing commenced, which was very considerably heightened upon one occasion by a plan of some of our wise-headed young gentlemen.   Being in want of amusement, they bethought them of priming the fire-engine, which happened to be standing on the poop, and after clapping a relay of hands ready to ply it to advantage, we uncovered and waited the approach of the boats.   No sooner were they within reach than off went the water-spout, which fell 'alike on the just and the unjust,' for both the dockyard men and the spectators who came within its compass got a good ducking.   This prank created an infernal confusion, and our trick having been twigged by the first lieutenant, the chief actors in this notable exploit were ordered up to the mast-head to enjoy their frolic for a few hours, which evidently much gratified the unfortunate sufferers from the effects of the operation."

According to an article in the *Times* of July 25, 1815, quoted by Mr. Ashton, " Napoleon at first wanted to make conditions with Captain Maitland as to his future treatment, but the British officer very properly declared that he must refer him upon this subject to his Government."   The midshipman says :—" As the time drew near when the resolution of the Government might be expected, the greatest anxiety began to manifest itself among the refugees." At length the fatal news arrived; the determination of the Government was officially communicated to Napoleon, and all was gloom and misery; and the writer adds:—"From that hour to the day of his leaving the ship, Napoleon never again appeared on deck."

"Maitland seemed to feel his situation a very disagreeable one. He saw," remarks the writer, "that his own conduct was not approved of by the narrow-minded Government.[1] He received strict orders only to treat Napoleon with the respect due to a general officer, and in future he was simply to be styled General Buonaparte.

"Maitland," he continues, "knowing how he stood with 'the powers that be,' was determined not to commit himself by accepting of any present of value from Napoleon, as he knew it would be directly made a handle of to injure his character as a British officer. He therefore, I believe, refused to accept of a gold snuff-box tendered him by the Emperor as a mark of his esteem."

Orders came on the 4th of August for the *Bellerophon* "to weigh and join the *Northumberland,* which was the ship in which Napoleon was to take

[1] Apparently, from a passage in Mr. J. Wolseley's second letter, some unpleasant comments were also made upon Sir Henry Hotham's conduct; and, from the midshipman's account, Captain Maitland only followed Sir Henry's example in treating Napoleon as an Emperor.

his passage to St. Helena." The midshipman of the *Bellerophon* says :—" We left Plymouth Sound in company with the *Tonnant*, bearing the flag of Admiral Lord Keith, and on the 6th we came to an anchor off Barry-head, there to wait the arrival of the *Northumberland*, which was hourly expected. She made her appearance in the course of the day, and after due salutes from both admirals' ships, in which noisy greeting we of course joined—for we are very polite at sea, in our own thundering way —she took up her station close by us. Towards evening Lord Keith came on board of us, and had a long personal interview with Napoleon in the cabin, which, we may judge, was not of the pleasantest nature, . . . and the 7th was appointed for Napoleon leaving the ship."

The writer remarks that the 7th " was a dull, cloudy, sunless day, and every countenance was overcast with gloom " ; and adds :—" We had not seen the Emperor for a week." He continues :— " Lord Keith, Admiral Cockburn, and Captain Ross came on board about eleven o'clock ; and it was intimated to Napoleon that they were ready to conduct him on board of the *Northumberland*. A general's guard of marines was drawn up on the quarter-deck to receive him as he came out of the cabin ; while part of his suite, and we officers, were ranged about, anxiously waiting the appearance of the future exile of St. Helena.

" Napoleon was long in attending to the intimation of the admirals; and upon Cockburn's becoming impatient, and remarking to old Lord Keith that he should be put in mind, Keith replied, ' No, no ; much greater men than either you or I have waited longer for him before now ; let him take his time, let him take his time.'

" At length Napoleon appeared, but oh, how sadly changed from the time we had last seen him upon deck ! Though quite plain, he was scrupulously cleanly in his person and dress, but that had been forgotten ; his clothes were ill put on, his beard unshaved, and his countenance pale and haggard. There was a want of firmness in his gait, his brow was overcast, and his whole visage bespoke the deepest melancholy ; and it needed but a glance to convince the most careless observer that Napoleon considered himself a doomed man. In this trying hour, however, he lost not his courtesy or presence of mind ; instinctively he raised his hat to the guard of marines when they presented arms as he passed ; slightly inclined his head, and even smiled, to us officers as he passed through us ; returned the salute of the admirals with calm dignity, and walking up to Captain Maitland, addressed him with great eagerness for nearly ten minutes.

" The purport of his speech to Captain Maitland was thanking him, his officers, and ship's company for the polite attention he had received while on board of the *Bellerophon*, which he should ever hold in kind remembrance. Something more he would have said after the first pause, and a feeling of deep emotion laboured in his face and swelled his breast; he looked earnestly in Maitland's face for a moment, as if about to renew his speech, but utterance seemed denied, and slightly moving his hat in salutation, he turned to Savary and L'Allemand, who were not allowed to accompany him to St. Helena, and spoke to them for a few minutes."

The writer speaks also of the dead silence in the ship during this scene, and says that, "had a pin fallen from one of the tops on the deck, I am convinced it would have been heard; and to any one who has known the general buzz of one of our seventy-fours, even at the quietest hour, it is a proof how deeply the attention of every man was riveted. Before leaving the ship Napoleon turned to us on the quarter-deck, once more waved his hand in token of adieu, took hold of the man-ropes, and walked down the side, taking his seat in the *Northumberland's* barge between Lord Keith and Admiral Cockburn.

"On looking back to the ship, he saw every head that could get stuck out of a port gazing after him; even the rough countenances of the men bespoke a sympathy for his cruel fate, and, apparently conscious of their feelings, the exiled chief again lifted his hat and inclined his head to the gazing ship's company."

The *Bellerophon*, like the *Superb*, was very shortly

afterwards paid off; and although the opinions of the young midshipman of the first-mentioned vessel seem to have been much influenced by the "fascination" which, according to Mr. John Wolseley, was exercised by the Emperor Napoleon upon all those who were about him, he makes the following remark :—"Clear of the Emperor and his suite, we felt as if let out of prison ourselves, for we had been everything but prisoners from the moment of our arrival in England." But he adds :—" Somehow or other the ship got coupled up with the name of Napoleon, and to be friendly to that great name and to belong to the *Bellerophon* was considered one and the same thing."

I am afraid the reader may think this account of the three weeks spent by Napoleon on board the *Bellerophon* is somewhat out of place in a memoir of Admiral Wolseley. But the extremely graphical descriptions given by the midshipman, when combined with the well‑written letters of Mr. Wolseley, form such a complete account of an interesting period in the life of the Emperor that I think it would have been a pity to have excluded them from this chapter. I have only to add that I hope the reader is of the same opinion, and will kindly consider the interest of the subject a sufficient excuse for this very long digression.

With the prospect of a peace, likely to be permanent, there was in the latter part of 1815 a general rush of English people to the Continent;

and Admiral and Mrs. Wolseley, shortly after these events, went abroad for the winter, as appears from the following note, written in a very shaky hand by old Mrs. Ricketts, sister of Lord St. Vincent :—

"ROCHETTS, *October 20th.*

" I cannot omit to thank you my dear Admiral, for the very kind lines with which you favored me. No mark of your remembrance is thrown away.

" I cannot forbear to regret, with my young people, the loss we are I fear to experience losing your society for many months, which at my advanced age may never be retrieved. Whilst I regret dear Mrs. Wolseley has been seriously ill, it is a comfort you keep free from Gout. Health and promotion I trust will be the meed of your most promising Son ; one regrets the separation from his kind friend Admiral Sir Henry Hotham, whose attention was really Parental. Ld. St. Vincent, who desires me to make his best regards, was gratified by seeing he had called in Mortimer Street.

" The private and the public accounts from France fluctuate ; one cannot divine how affairs will be reduced to permanent order.

" Your young friends unite in every good wish, with, my dear Admiral, your affectionate old friend, MARY RICKETTS."

Admiral Wolseley and his family, I think, returned to Ghent, and spent that winter and the following spring there. The Admiral was, I believe, also accompanied by his eldest son, Mr. John Wolseley, who was at that time in rather delicate health, the result of an attack of bronchitis, brought on by a severe cold, in consequence of which, I think, he did not rejoin his ship until the end of the spring of 1816, when his father and the rest of the family returned to their home in Bath.

CHAPTER IX

NEXT in date among the old letters appears some interesting correspondence about the attack made by the fleet upon Algiers on the afternoon of the 27th of August 1816, in which the Admiral's eldest son, Mr. John Wolseley, greatly distinguished himself. He was at that time still serving as midshipman on board the *Superb*, seventy-four guns, commanded by Captain Ekins; and having been most favourably mentioned in the despatches written immediately after the battle by Lord Exmouth, the commander-in-chief, he was at once promoted to the rank of lieutenant.

However, before giving copies of two letters that were doubtless very gratifying to Admiral and Mrs. Wolseley, one written by Lord Exmouth and the other by Captain Ekins, I take some extracts with an interesting account of the siege of Algiers from the Appendix to Dr. Campbell's "Naval History," in which that author says :—

"We conclude these volumes by the official account of an exploit equal to any previously committed to these pages in danger, skill, bravery, and success. Lord Exmouth had arranged a treaty with the Dey of Algiers previous to his quitting the Mediterranean, but even before his arrival in England accounts had been received of a horrible massacre which took place at Bona. Immediately his squadron was refitted and strengthened, and sailed for Algiers. During his stay at Gibraltar he accepted the assistance of a Dutch squadron under Admiral Van de Capellan, and having made all his arrangements, on the 14th of August the united squadrons put to sea." Dr. Campbell then gives the names of all the vessels, and from the list it appears the English had altogether twenty-one ships, and the Dutch only six. Lord Exmouth's flag-ship, the *Queen Charlotte*, was a ship of 110 guns; the *Superb*, the *Minden*, and the *Albion* were ships of seventy-four guns; the rest, including five gun-boats that joined the fleet at Gibraltar, were all smaller vessels. And the Dutch had four ships of forty-four guns, one of thirty, and another of eighteen guns. Dr. Campbell then gives a copy of Lord Exmouth's letter to the First Lord of the Admiralty, written the day after the battle, and as a most graphical account of the engagement is given by his lordship, I take a few passages from his despatch, which he commences as follows :—

"'QUEEN CHARLOTTE,' ALGIERS BAY,
Aug. 28, 1816.

"SIR,—In all the vicissitudes of a long life of public service, no circumstance has ever produced on my mind such impressions of gratitude and joy as the event of yesterday. To have been one of the humble instruments, in the hands of Divine Providence, for bringing to reason a ferocious government, and destroying for ever the insufferable and horrid system of Christian slavery, can never cease to be a source of delight and heartfelt comfort to every individual happy enough to be employed in it. I may, I hope, be permitted, under such impressions, to offer my sincere congratulations to their lordships on the complete success which attended the gallant efforts of his Majesty's fleet in their attack upon Algiers of yesterday, and the happy result produced from it on this day by the signature of peace."

Lord Exmouth continues : — "Would to God that in the attainment of this object I had not deeply to lament the severe loss of so many gallant officers and men ; they have profusely bled in a contest which has been marked by proofs of such devoted heroism as would rouse every noble feeling, did I dare indulge in relating them.

"Their lordships will already have been informed, by his Majesty's sloop *Jasper*, of my proceedings up to the 14th instant, on which day I broke ground from Gibraltar after a vexatious detention, by a foul wind, of four days.

" The fleet, complete in all its points, with the

addition of five gun-boats fitted at Gibraltar, departed in the highest spirits, and with the most favourable prospect of reaching the port of their destination in three days ; but an adverse wind destroyed the expectation of an early arrival, which was the more anxiously looked for by myself, in consequence of hearing, the day I sailed from Gibraltar, that a large army had been assembled, and that very considerable additional works were throwing up, not only on both flanks of the city, but also immediately about the entrance of the mole ; from this I was apprehensive that my intention of making that point my principal object of attack had been discovered to the Dey by the same means he had heard of the expedition. This intelligence was, on the following night, greatly confirmed by the captain of the *Prometheus*, which I had despatched to Algiers some time before, to endeavour to get away the consul. Captain Dashwood had with difficulty succeeded in bringing away, disguised in midshipman's uniform, the consul's wife and daughter, leaving a boat to bring off their infant child coming down in a basket with the surgeon, who thought he had composed it, but it unhappily cried in the gateway, and, in consequence, the surgeon, three midshipmen, and, in all, eighteen persons, were seized and confined as slaves in the usual dungeons. The child was sent off next morning by the Dey, and as a solitary instance of his humanity, it ought to be recorded by me.

"Captain Dashwood further confirmed, that about forty thousand men had been brought down from the interior, and all the janisaries called in from distant garrisons, and that they were indefatigably employed in their batteries, gun-boats, &c., and everywhere strengthening the sea-defences.

"The ships were all in port, and between forty and fifty gun and mortar boats were ready, with several more in forward repair. The Dey had closely confined the consul, and refused either to give him up or promise his personal safety; nor would he hear a word respecting the officers and men seized in the boats of the *Prometheus*.

"From the continuance of adverse winds and calms, the land to the westward of Algiers was not made before the 26th, and the next morning at day-break the fleet was advanced in sight of the city, though not so near as I had intended. As the ships were becalmed, I embraced this opportunity of despatching a boat under cover of the *Severn*, with a flag of truce, and the demands I had to make, in the name of his Royal Highness the Prince Regent, on the Dey of Algiers, directing the officer to wait two or three hours for the Dey's answer, at which time, if no reply was sent, he was to return to the flag-ship; he was met near the mole by the captain of the port, who, on being told the answer was expected in one hour, replied that it was impossible; the officer then said he would wait two or three hours; he then observed two hours was quite sufficient.

"The fleet at this time, by the springing up of the sea-breeze, had reached the bay, and were preparing the boats and flotilla for service until near two o'clock, when, observing my officer was returning with the signal flying that no answer had been received for upwards of three hours, I instantly made the signal to know if the ships were all ready, which being answered in the affirmative, the *Queen Charlotte* bore up, followed up by the fleet, for their appointed stations; the flag, leading in the prescribed order, was anchored in the entrance of the mole, at about fifty yards distance. At this moment not a gun had been fired, and I began to expect a full compliance with the terms which had been for so many hours in their hands; at this period of profound silence a shot was fired at us from the mole, and two at the ships to the northward then following; this was promptly returned by the *Queen Charlotte*, who was then lashing to the main-mast of a brig, fast to the shore in the mouth of the mole, and which we had steered for as the guide to our position.

"Thus commenced a fire as animated and well supported as, I believe, was ever witnessed, from a quarter before three until nine, without intermission, and which did not cease altogether until half-past eleven.

"The ships immediately following me were admirably and coolly taking their stations, with a precision even beyond my most sanguine hope; and never did the British flag receive, on any occasion, more zealous and honourable support. To look farther on the line than immediately round me was perfectly impossible, but so well grounded was my confidence in the gallant officers I had the honour to command, that my mind was left perfectly free to attend to other objects, and I knew them in their stations only by the destructive effect of their fire upon the walls and batteries to which they were opposed.

"I had about this time the satisfaction of seeing Vice-Admiral Van Capellan's flag in the station I had assigned to him, and soon after, at intervals, the remainder of his frigates keeping up a well-supported fire on the flanking batteries he had offered to cover us from, as it had not been in my power, for want of room, to bring him in the front of the mole.

"About sunset I received a message from Rear-Admiral Milne, conveying to me the severe loss the *Impregnable* was sustaining, having then one hundred and fifty killed and wounded, and requesting I would, if possible, send him a frigate to divert some of the fire he was under.

"The *Glasgow*, near me, immediately weighed, but

the wind had been driven away by the cannonade, and she was obliged to anchor again, having obtained rather a better position than before.

"I had at this time sent orders to the explosion vessel, under the charge of Lieutenant Fleming and Mr. Parker, by Captain Reade, of the Engineers, to bring her into the mole; but the rear-admiral having thought she would do him essential service if exploded under the battery in his front, I sent orders to this vessel to that effect, which were executed. I desired also the rear-admiral might be informed that, many of the enemy's ships being now in flames, and certain of the destruction of the whole, I considered I had executed the most important part of my instructions, and should make every preparation for withdrawing the ships, and desired he would do so as soon as possible with his division.

"There were awful moments during the conflict which I cannot now attempt to describe, occasioned by firing the ships so near us, and I had long resisted the eager entreaties of several around me to make the attempt upon the outer frigate, distant about one hundred yards, which at length I gave in to, and Major Gossett, by my side, who had been eager to land his corps of miners, pressed me most anxiously for permission to accompany Lieutenant Richards in this ship's barge. The frigate was instantly boarded, and in ten minutes in a perfect blaze. A gallant young midshipman, in rocket - boat No. 8, although forbidden, was led by his ardent spirit to follow in support of the barge, in which he was desperately wounded, his brother officer killed, and nine of his crew. The barge, by rowing more rapidly, had suffered less, and lost but two.

" The enemy's batteries around my division were about ten o'clock silenced, and in a state of perfect ruin and dilapidation, and the fire of the ships was reserved as much as possible, to save powder, and reply to a few guns now and then bearing upon us, although a fort on the upper angle of the city, on which our guns could not be brought to bear, continued to annoy the ships by shot and shells during the whole time.

" Providence at this interval gave to my anxious wishes the usual land wind, common in this bay, and my expectations were completed. We were all hands employed warping and towing off, and by the help of the light air the whole were under sail, and came to anchor out of reach of shells about two in the morning, after twelve hours' incessant labour.

" The flotilla of mortar, gun, and rocket boats, under the direction of their respective artillery officers, shared, to the fullest extent of their power, in the honours of this day, and performed good service; it was by their fire all the ships in the port (with the exception of the outer frigate) were in flames, which extended rapidly over the whole arsenal, store-houses, and gun-boats, exhibiting a spectacle of awful grandeur and interest no pen can describe."

The rest of Lord Exmouth's despatch is taken up by details of the way in which the service was performed, and in commendation of the officers and seamen employed in it. In the end of the letter he says :—" I am happy to say Captains Ekins and Coode are doing well, as also the whole of the wounded." And he adds :—" By accounts from the shore, I understand the enemy's loss in killed and wounded is between six and seven thousand men." The loss on the side of the English was 128 killed and 600 wounded ; on that of the Dutch, 13 killed and 52 wounded.

The result gained by this great victory was, that on the 28th of August, the day on which Lord Exmouth's despatch was written, the Dey signed a treaty containing a declaration, "that in the event of future wars with any European Power, not any of the prisoners should be consigned to slavery, but treated with all humanity as prisoners of war, until regularly exchanged, according to European practice." And no less than "one thousand and eighty-three Christian slaves" who were at Algiers were released, and were shortly after forwarded by Lord Exmouth "in British transports to their respective countries."[1]

---

[1] Another writer places the number of those who were liberated at 3000.

Perhaps the reader may consider this long account of the siege of Algiers rather out of place, on the grounds that Admiral Wolseley was not present. But I think Lord Exmouth's account is so interesting that it would be a pity to have omitted it. And as Mr. John Wolseley was serving on board of one of the vessels engaged, and greatly distinguished himself on the occasion, his father must necessarily have taken the deepest interest in this event, and have been much gratified by the letters he received concerning it. The first of these letters is one from Lord Exmouth :—

"'QUEEN CHARLOTTE,' AT SEA,
"25*th Sept.* 1816.

" MY DEAR ADMIRAL,—You will very readily believe that I was so fully occupied in the preparation of my fleet that I had not five minutes to spare to make any other arrangement for your son, than leaving him where he then was on board the *Superb*. The flag-ship was crowded even as thick as three in a Bed. I should not have lost sight of him had any opportunity offered to serve him ; but the service ending in only one fight when I expected half a dozen, left me no other way of showing my respect for you, than that of marking against his name in the list I have laid before Melville how deserving he is of promotion. Your own weight added to my Testimony will I hope secure his Advancement. He is spoken very

highly of by Capt. Ekins and appears a remark-
able fine young man ; his being wounded will add
to his claim, altho' it was but very slight. Wishing
you every enjoyment your happy retirement affords,
and which I sigh for, believe me my dear Wolseley
ever your faithful Servant,   EXMOUTH."

Letter No. 2.

" Lord Melville presents his compliments to Vice
Admiral Wolseley and has the honor to acquaint
him that his Son Mr. J. H. Wolseley has been
promoted to the rank of Lieutenant by a Commission dated the 13th of this month.
"ADMIRALTY, *26th September* 1816."

The next letter is one written by Mr. John
Wolseley to Captain Grace, and which was afterwards sent by the latter to Admiral Wolseley :—

" 'SUPERB,' PLYH., *Oct.* 6, 1816.

" MY DEAR SIR,—No doubt you think I am a
very pretty fellow for not keeping my promise to
write to you from Algiers, but really I had hardly
time to write a few lines to my father which I
am sorry to find he has never received. *You* can
conceive the state a ship must have been in after
an action of such long continuance and how impossible it must have been for me, rendered helpless
by a wound in the leg, to bustle about. It was with

the greatest difficulty I procured *one* sheet of paper.
But I will now endeavour to tell you everything
which I think you *could not* collect from the public
dispatches ; though as a mid's sphere of observation
is rather limited you will excuse the *Superb's* being
in a great measure the Burden of my song. Indeed
I had too much to do in her to take much notice
of the motions of other ships. Every body must
admire the *cool* manner in which Lord Ex. ran in,
and we may attribute our success entirely to our
going so very close. The faults on the part of the
Algerines were as follows—1st, being so sure of
destroying us all that they did not fire until we
had taken our stations. 2nd, not depressing their
guns sufficiently (perhaps they could not). 3rd,
firing landgridge, which did not penetrate our sides,
instead of round. And 4thly, not firing red hot
shot—had they done *any one* of these—I shudder
when I think of the probable consequences. Their
batteries were the finest I ever saw and a skill displayed in their positions that appears quite beyond
the knowledge of Musselman Engineers. Some
of the mole forts put me in mind of Blockhouse,
Portsmouth, but they were I think of better materials than the latter as the shot *sank* into them.
Their guns were all Brass, in excellent order as far
as we could judge — and of immense caliber in
some places. The sponges, etc., were all stuck up
over the parapet when we were going in. This
ship anchored with two anchors ahead and two

astern — two of the cables backed with chains.
We were about the same distance with the Adml.
from the works. I was wounded in the leg the
first broadside by a splinter from a shot that came
in on the Quarter Deck; it, however, I am happy
to say was not so bad as to oblige me to leave
my quarters until a long time afterwards. To
give you some idea of the number of shot that
passed over us—one ensign was shot away, and
the second had 9 or 10 round shot through it
besides grape and musket Balls ; we counted above
80 holes in the foretopsail (clewed up). Only 2 or
3 of our *small* spars escaped unhurt, and only 4
ropes left uncut in the ship of any description,—
one of which, the Topmast spring stay alone prevented our mainmast going over the stern. It had
9 shot through it; two of them either 68's or 42's.
Had not the breeze been very light, we must have
lost our sticks. Our Hull not materially damaged
though we have a good deal of chain shot, Lang-
ridge and *glass* sticking in our sides. If we had
come too further out we must have been *sunk* or
at least have suffered in the same manner as *Impregnable*, as the shot that passed over us would
in that case have told on our hull. This ship fired
260 Barrels of Powder, and 81 Tons of shot;
though we slackened our fire much, latterly, to
save ammunition. We went out under the long
Topsail, Spritsail, and Main Topmast stay sail.
Queen Charlotte escaped being burnt almost by a

miracle. Towards the conclusion the scene was grand and awful beyond description. The enemy's blazing frigates and our shells and rockets illumined the whole Bay. The Algerines fought desperately. When driven from their guns they fired musketry, and attempted in the most daring way to extinguish the fire in their ships. I understand in a boat sunk by the *Leander* they went down waving their sabres. We can none of us be too thankful for our safety and success. *Our shot were directed* because our cause was just. I believe I have now told you everything worth mentioning, — at least that I can recollect. My wound was of no great consequence and is quite well ; it did not however heal until we got into the cold weather. There is little doubt of my being promoted, as Lord Exmouth told me I was on his private list which he will give to Lord Melville. I shall then go to Bath where my father is. In all this long story I have forgotten to thank you for your kind letter of July 25th, which I received the day we sailed. I am truly sorry you were not with us, but it cannot be helped. I suppose this will find you in Scotland—I trust in good health. The *Euphrates* came into Gibraltar the day we sailed, but as she was under Quarantine I could not see Charles Freemantle. It was very provoking.[1]

"I must now conclude this, perhaps you will

---

[1] Afterwards Admiral Sir Charles Home Fremantle, G.C.B., who was probably at that time serving as a midshipman in the *Euphrates*.

think *too long* Epistle, with the assurance that I
remain yours sincerely,   " J. WOLSELEY.

" Best Compts. to Capt. Leith.

" My father and mother are well, and would I
am sure join with me in best wishes for your
happiness, did they know I was writing to you."

The next letter is one written by Captain Ekins
to Admiral Wolseley :—

      "'SUPERB,' HAMOAZE, *Octr.* 14*th* 1816.

" MY DEAR SIR,—I cannot sufficiently thank
you for your kind and most flattering congratulations upon the success of our late expedition, and
it cannot but be grateful to our feelings, to see that
our exertions are so highly estimated by officers of
Rank and ability in our own profession, and who,
like yourself, are so well qualified to judge of the
degree of skill and risk necessary for so desperate
a service.

" It is with equal truth and pleasure, that I can
bear my testimony to your Son's steady and gallant
conduct in the action ; and to add a circumstance,
which his modesty may have tempted him to con-
ceal ; as honourable to himself, as proud and gratifying to his Parents ; it is, that he would not leave
his quarters until he was positively *commanded by
me*, and then with evident reluctance, and he had
continued working at his guns some time after he

received his wound, and it was communicated to me by the Lieutt. at his quarters, when upon seeing a good deal of blood upon his trousers, I immediately ordered him down to the Surgeon.

" I am extremely happy to find the Admiralty (or rather Ld. Melville) have rewarded his services with promotion, and this is the more satisfactory to all parties since it does not in the least interfere with any other young man I have been called upon to nominate from this ship, but which, from being confined to *one only* of my own, I cannot but consider is a very inadequate mark of their Lordships' approbation of our services, and of which very limited patronage, I cannot but feel greatly mortified and disappointed.   Your Son tells me he has this day received his Commission, but that as his Pay List will not be returned until Thursday, he will be detained here a few days longer.   Allow me to offer you and Mrs. Wolseley my sincere and hearty congratulations on this event, and with my best regards remain, my dear Sir, your faithful obliged and very Hble. Servant,   CHARLES EKINS."

This letter, which must have been a very gratifying one to Admiral and Mrs. Wolseley, closes the correspondence on the subject of the siege of Algiers.

The end of the following year, 1817, found Admiral Wolseley and his family still living in Bath ; and some members of the royal family at

that time honoured the town with a visit.   Mr.
Ashton, in his "Social England under the Regency," says :—"The health of Queen Charlotte was
beginning to fail, and her physicians recommended
her to go to Bath for the waters ; and she accordingly repaired thither in November, accompanied
by the Duke of Clarence."

The evening the royal party arrived, there was
a gala performance at the theatre, at which the
Duke of Clarence was present.   Admiral and Mrs.
Wolseley also went to the play, and took their
eldest daughter to it ; and the following morning,
the Admiral, having heard that the Queen was going
to make her first appearance at the Pump-Room,
and that all the *beau monde* of Bath were going to it,
took his daughter there also.   They were walking
about the room talking to the different friends they
met, when the Duke of Clarence came up and
claimed acquaintance with him ; and it was doubtless
on that occasion that his Royal Highness reminded
Admiral Wolseley of their first meeting, when he,
the Duke, was doing duty as a midshipman on
board the *Hebe*, and was sent in command of a boat
from that vessel to assist in towing the *Trusty* out
of Spithead.

After he had been talking for some little time with
the Admiral and his daughter, the Duke asked the
latter if she had been presented to his "mother";
and upon her replying that she had not had that
honour, he said, "Then come with me and I

will present you to her." The room was densely
crowded, and they had to walk to the far end of
it; but two gentlemen carrying wands went before
them making way for them to pass, and the people
who were nearest stood back very respectfully.

Queen Charlotte, who was standing near the
pump with a glass of water in her hand, turned
round with a pleasant smile on her face when the
Duke spoke to her, and bowed very graciously to
Miss Wolseley; and her Majesty and the Princess
Elizabeth, to whom Miss Wolseley was also presented, talked with her in a very easy and affable
manner for some minutes.

Admiral Wolseley was rather surprised at the
Duke's recognition of him, as they had only met
once, and a great many years had passed since their
meeting. He spoke of this to a friend, who told
him that his Royal Highness had taken notice of
the little family party at the theatre the evening
before, and had sent one of his gentlemen-in-waiting
to him to find out who they were.

An incident that occurred during the Queen's
visit to Bath is related by Mr. Ashton, who probably took the account from some ancient local
paper. "The following anecdote of her sojourn,"
he writes, "is dated ' Bath, November 28th.' The
Queen wishing to ride through Prior Park, the
property of John Thomas, a very rich Quaker, a
footman was sent forward to the house to ask leave
for the gates to be opened. Mr. Thomas received

the Queen very respectfully at the park gate, and addressed her as follows : ' Charlotte, I hope thee is very well. I am glad to see thee in my park ; thou art very welcome at any time, and I shall feel proud in opening my gates for thy pleasure. I hope thou receives benefit from the Bath waters. I wish thee well.' " This short speech, though rather oddly expressed, was as much to the point as such addresses usually are, and no doubt her Majesty thought it more amusing than the generality of them.

At the time she was staying in Bath there were a great many naval officers living there, and it was decided by them that they should join in giving a dinner-party in honour of H.R.H. the Duke of Clarence, who was then admiral of the fleet, and who was, of course, to be the guest of the evening. Vice-Admiral Wolseley was the senior officer then living in Bath, and he was consequently elected president on the great occasion.

Among the Admiral's papers there is a plan of the dinner-table, with the names of all those who were present, and the order in which they were placed. From this list it appears that, with the Duke of Clarence, who, of course, sat at the right side of Admiral Wolseley, who presided at the head of the table, there were two gentlemen-in-waiting on his Royal Highness—Lieutenant-Colonel Miles and Lieutenant-Colonel Cowper. And of the Prince's loyal hosts there were fifty-two present, including the president and Vice-Admiral Sotheby, who acted as vice-president and sat at the foot of the table. The other flag-officers whose names are given in the list were the following :—Vice-Admirals Sir William Haywood, Sir D. Gould, Mark Robinson, and Crawley ; Rear - Admirals Sir William Hotham, Otway, Ballard, Taylor, T. Wolley, Macknamara, and Dacres. Twenty-two captains were present at the entertainment, and all the other officers there were respectively commanders and lieutenants in the navy.[1]

At the back of the paper appears also a long list of the toasts that were drunk on the festive occasion, with the names of the airs played by the band after each. The health of the poor old King, it appears, and that of " His Serene Highness Prince Leopold of Saxe-Coburg," who had recently lost his wife, the Princess Charlotte of Wales, were drunk in silence.[2] The company were all standing while these toasts, and the healths of other members of the royal family, the army, and that of the Duke of Wellington, were being honoured. The air mentioned as having been played by the band after the health of " His Royal Highness the Prince Regent," and also that of " Her Majesty, our most gracious Queen," was " God save the King." After the

---

[1] Among the names of the captains appears that of John Maitland, who was probably the officer in command of the *Bellerophon* to whom Napoleon surrendered himself two years before.

[2] Princess Charlotte of Wales, Duchess of Saxe-Coburg, died on the 7th November 1817.

health of the "illustrious guest, His Royal Highness, the Admiral of the Fleet," "Rule Britannia" was played; and the health of the Duke of Wellington was appropriately followed by the air of "See the Conquering Hero Comes."

There is no memorandum of the date, but I think this banquet took place very shortly after the arrival of the royal party at Bath. The day after it, Admiral Wolseley happened to meet the Duke of Clarence, who was taking a walk. His Royal Highness stopped to speak to him, and asked the Admiral to join him; and I believe, on several other occasions afterwards, he had the honour of accompanying the Prince in his walks about the town and its neighbourhood.

When his Royal Highness was leaving Bath, he advised the Admiral to send his youngest son, Cosby Wolseley, to Sandhurst, and said that he would get a commission for him himself. At that time the Duke's very kind offer was not accepted by Admiral Wolseley, as he was not then decided upon placing his son in the army; and Mrs. Wolseley, it appears, was most anxious that their youngest boy, when old enough to do so, should enter the Church and become a clergyman.

CHAPTER X

AMONG the letters preserved by Admiral Wolseley
are five, written to him by the Duke of Clarence.
Some of these letters, or rather notes, were
written many years after their meeting at Bath,
and they all more or less show the high estimation
in which Admiral Wolseley was held by the Duke.
Excepting, perhaps, for this, and from the circumstance that the writer was afterwards king of
England, there is no great interest in the letters
themselves.

The date of the first is not given. But from
what the Duke says in it about his "union," it
seems to have been written early in the year 1818,
shortly before the 11th of June, on which day the
Duke was married to her Serene Highness Princess
Adelaide, the eldest daughter of the Duke of Saxe-
Meiningen. The following is a copy of the little
note, which was evidently written in reply to one
from Admiral Wolseley :—

"BRIGHTON, *Tuesday, Noon.*

"DEAR SIR,—Your kind letter of 25th instant
has just reached me. I return you my sincere
thanks for your obliging enquiries. I have not

the smallest idea of giving up either *the Union* or *my life* but of remaining for a *very long time*, dear Sir, yours invariably   WILLIAM."

Next in date, in the package of old letters, comes a note written to the Admiral, in which another was enclosed, that can scarcely have failed to have given pleasure to Mr. John Wolseley's father and mother.   Before giving copies, however, I think I should say a few words about the gentleman who had so kindly sent the other letter to them.   The Hon. Henry Blackwood, afterwards Vice-Admiral, and created a baronet, was in 1785 placed as a midshipman on board the *Trusty*, where he served for four years under the command of Admiral Wolseley, who was then captain of that vessel.   Sir Henry Blackwood's subsequent naval career was a most distinguished one.   On various occasions he rendered very important services, and as captain of the *Euryalus*, took part in the battle of Trafalgar, and the despatches announcing that glorious victory were brought home by him.

On the outside of his note, addressed to " Vice-Adml. Wolseley, 5 Norfolk Crescent, Bath," is the date " January 1819 " :—

" MY DEAR ADMIRAL,—As I feel that it must give you and Mrs. W. great pleasure, I can't resist the transmission of the annexed which you may keep or burn as you please.—Always most truly yours,

" HY. BLACKWOOD."

The note enclosed was one from Admiral Sir Henry Hotham, in whose flag-ship Mr. John Wolseley had formerly served for some years as a midshipman :—

"ADMIRALTY, *Jany.* 15*th.*

"MY DEAR BLACKWOOD,—As Captains have the privilege of naming their own Senior Lieutenants, and as Mr. Gore has been removed from the *Scout* unknown to Captain Ramsden, the Board think he may be indulged with the choice of a Successor, and I have written to ask him if there should be any officer in the Mediterranean who he would wish for, or any friend in England to apply for. If he has none, I shall be glad to attend to your recommendation of Lieut. King, and will note him.

"Young Wolseley is *everything* that you *can have heard* of him, or think *can be said of him,* and I assure you there is not a finer, or more amiable young man, in existence; and if any opportunity should offer for sending him to you in India, with advantage to him, I will not neglect, should it be his wish, and that of his Father.

"I believe the *Rochfort* is quite ready, and may sail at any time; the Captain has his orders, and the ship is only wind-bound.—Believe me, Dear Blackwood, very faithfully yours,

"HENRY HOTHAM."

Sir Henry Blackwood's kindness in sending this note to them was doubtless fully appreciated by Admiral and Mrs. Wolseley. Like most of the officers who had ever served under the Admiral, Sir Henry Blackwood seems to have felt the warmest affection for his old commander. Ample evidence of this affection, both as regards Sir Henry himself and that also of other officers, is to be found among the letters preserved by Admiral Wolseley.

On the 12th of August 1819 Vice-Admiral Wolseley was promoted to the rank of admiral, and was placed on the list of officers of that degree included in the Blue Squadron.

In the year 1819 there seems to have been very great depression in trade in England, and in consequence there was much distress and discontent. In many parts of the country very serious riots took place, got up by people whose opinions were apparently similar to those of the "Chartists," of somewhat later date.

Sir Charles Wolseley, the seventh baronet of the elder branch of the family, who had succeeded to the Staffordshire estate about two years before that time, was apparently a man not gifted with very much sense, and, to the great annoyance of Admiral Wolseley and of his other relations, he made himself very conspicuous as a leader of these people.

A great many years after the period of which I have just been writing, old Sir Richard Wolseley, the fourth baronet of the Irish branch, told the

P

Admiral's daughter, Mrs. Innes, that he had spent part of the summer of 1819 in London, and when on his way there, having had a rough passage in crossing, he remained in Liverpool for a night, and started for London next day. The morning he left Liverpool he noticed that the streets through which he passed were crowded with people of the artisan and working class, who were apparently all wending their way in one direction. Having asked the postillion if anything was going on in the town, he was told that a great political meeting was then taking place; and a few minutes afterwards they entered a square so crowded with people that it was almost impossible to move even at a foot-pace, and his carriage, an open phaeton, very shortly came to a stand-still a few yards from a sort of rough platform formed of casks set up on end with planks laid across them; and, to the great astonishment and disgust of Sir Richard, who had not at that time heard that Sir Charles had joined the rebels, he discovered that the orator who was standing on the top of this erection addressing a most revolutionary speech to the assembled mob was no other than his own cousin.

It was probably Sir Charles Wolseley's first appearance in public as a supporter of the discontented party, and the positive discovery made by him that he had at least one most unsympathetic listener among the audience seems to have had an astonishing effect upon his nerves. He did not at first see Sir Richard; but when, in the course of his speech, he chanced to look towards the side of the square where he was, and caught sight of his cousin sitting in his carriage within a few yards of himself, to Sir Richard's great amusement, he got very red, and was so confused that he could scarcely continue his speech, seemed to have completely lost the thread of his discourse, and for some minutes did not succeed in regaining his composure.

Although the meeting involuntarily attended by Sir Richard was perhaps the first at which Sir Charles publicly came forward as an advocate of the cause of the malcontents, it was certainly not the last time he appeared in that capacity; and in the month of December, apparently, from a letter written by the Duke of Clarence in reply to one from Admiral Wolseley, some severe comments were made by the Admiral upon Sir Charles's conduct in joining them; and he seems also at the same time to have expressed his own regret that a relation of his should continue to be so misguided.[1] The following is a copy of the Duke's letter :—

"St. James's, *Decr. 9th*, 1819.

"Dear Sir, — Yours of yesterday has just reached me and I lament to find you have been

[1] Sir Charles Wolseley was a second cousin of the Admiral.

so much indisposed; but trust you are fast recovering; everybody must lament the disturbed state of the country and particularly those few individuals who have relations foolish and wicked enough to join the disaffected: the conduct of Sir Charles Wolseley is inexplicable and I can easily conceive it must give you great concern to be related to a person who continues to mislead himself and others.

"I am most heartily glad to have returned to dear old England, and by care and attention have very considerably restored my health. I wish your son could have had the advantage of the Military College; but we must think in proper time of placing him in the army. For the present adieu and ever believe me, Dear Sir, yours sincerely,

"WILLIAM."

In the end of 1820 Admiral Wolseley took his family to Ghent for the winter, as it was thought that the change of air might be of use to Mrs. Wolseley, who had been for some time in very delicate health. In the early part of 1821, I think, they went to Brussels for a few weeks, but as Mrs. Wolseley became much more seriously ill they returned to Ghent; and, to the great grief of the Admiral and her family, she died there in the month of March.

After Mrs. Wolseley's death the Admiral returned to England with his daughters; and I find no record of the remaining months of that year, or any whatever of the following one, 1822. Next among the old papers appears a copy of a letter, evidently taken from one written by Admiral Wolseley to the Duke of Clarence. At the head of the copy—which, I think, is in the Admiral's handwriting—is the following :—

*"Letter sent by John dated 28 Feb. 1823,
To the Duke of Clarence.*

" SIR,—When at Bath your Royal Highness did me the honour to profess an interest in the welfare of my two sons the eldest of whom, (at that time in the *Superb* at Algiers,) you expressed a desire to see. I have long solicited employment for him, and now send him to London to try if his personal applications will be more successful than my letters ; and recollecting your Royal Highness's kindness I venture to write these few lines to recommend him to your notice. I have commanded him to pay his respects to you, feeling confident, that if it should happen to be in your Royal Highness's power to be of any service to him, he will not prove unworthy of your attentions. I hope to hear from my son a favourable account of your Royal Highness's health, and that it has not suffered during this severe winter, which has borne hardly on my gouty floor timbers.[1] With

---

[1] A nautical expression, used, I believe, for the planks which are laid on the lowest part of the framework of a vessel, and which are called by sailors the "floor timbers" of the ship.

every wish for your health and happiness, permit
me to subscribe myself with the most profound
respect, Your Royal Highness's much obliged and
most obedt. Humble Servt.,   W. W."

Shortly after that Mr. John Wolseley again
went to sea, and having been appointed one of
the lieutenants on board Admiral Sir George Eyre's
flag-ship, he was sent out to Rio Janeiro.

Towards the end of the year 1823 Admiral
Wolseley took his daughters over to Ireland, to
pay visits to some of their mother's relations,
and a great part of their time was spent with
Mrs. M^cc^Gwire, a sister of Mrs. Wolseley. This
lady was living near the village of Rostrevor, at
a place that had been bought by her late husband, who had formerly been a captain in the
navy.

Admiral Wolseley's youngest daughter had never
been in Ireland before; and his eldest had not, I
believe, been in that country since she was quite
a little child, when her father gave up command
of the Sea Fencibles and had settled in Bath.
Their first experience of travelling in Ireland was
by no means a pleasant one. They came down
from Dublin in the mail-coach, and just as they
were descending a very steep hill about half a
mile from Newry an accident occurred. One of
the horses fell and the carriage-pole got broken.
It was quite late in the evening, almost dark,

and the rain was coming down in torrents; but notwithstanding this the passengers were obliged to get out, and had to walk into Newry. Miss Sydney Wolseley, the Admiral's youngest daughter, unfortunately, had a very bad cold at the time, and to save her from getting her feet wet, her father took her up in his arms, and carried her the whole way into the town, where they passed the night, going on to Rostrevor next day.

The Admiral, who, I believe, had never been there before, took a great fancy to Rostrevor, and was much struck by the beauty of the surrounding scenery; and thinking, also, that it would be an advantage to his daughters to be settled near their aunt, he, shortly after their visit to Mrs. M\ :superscript:cc Gwire, decided on giving up his house in Bath, and upon coming over to live at Rostrevor. Accordingly, in the month of March 1824, he bought a little place in the village from his nephew, Mr. M\ :superscript:cc Gwire, who had some property there. The house was entirely remodelled; the offices were built and the gardens were laid out by Admiral Wolseley, who afterwards gave the little place the name of " The Anchorage "—a very appropriate one for the residence of a retired naval officer!

Next among the old letters appears a copy of the following letter written by Admiral Sir George Eyre to Admiral Wolseley. Mr. John Wolseley, apparently, was then on his way home, having

been obliged to return on account of his health
having failed, from the effects of the climate of
Rio Janeiro:—

"WELLESLEY, RIO JANEIRO,
"*Augst.* 11, 1826.

"MY DEAR SIR,—Your son will probably have
informed you before you receive this, of the necessity he has been under of leaving this Station,
and I cannot express how much I lament it; but
the season of the year, when this ship will probably
arrive in England, would make the risks greater
than could be justified, and the Surgeon has been,
for some time past, decidedly of that opinion; I
wish with all my heart, it had been in my power
to give him the rank he is so highly deserving of,
and to which he had so strong a claim, before he
left me, and it is not less on public grounds, than
his own account I feel the disappointment, for
with his highly cultivated mind, superior talents
and devotion to his profession, the greatest advantage to the service might be expected from
him.   I sincerely hope that a few months will
restore him to good health, and that I may have
the satisfaction of congratulating you on his promotion; his loss will be deeply felt by us all, for
it is not possible for a young man to be more
beloved and respected than he is.   I was very glad
to hear a pretty good account of yourself, and that
you were enabled to keep the enemy tolerably
under control.   I am feeling the effects of this

enervating climate, and look for my successor with anxious expectation.—I am, dear Sir, yours very faithfully, GEO. EYRE."

In the beginning of the year 1827 H.R.H. the Duke of Clarence was promoted to the rank of Lord High Admiral of England, and the following note was written by him in reply to Admiral Wolseley's congratulations upon that event :—

"LONDON, *April 25th*, 1827.

"DEAR SIR,—I have this day received yours of 22nd instant and thank you most sincerely for your kind congratulations on my appointment to this most arduous situation.

"I trust my conduct will ensure me the continuance of your good opinion and I ever remain yours most truly, WILLIAM."

Mr. John Wolseley was apparently much disappointed at not having got his promotion, and in one of his letters written to his father, I think, before he left Rio Janeiro, he remarked on the hardship of having served for eleven years as a lieutenant, while some other officers of the same rank had been promoted, though they had not served for nearly as long a time. After he came over to Ireland he evidently got his father to write to the Duke of Clarence on the

subject, and the following very kind little note was
the Duke's reply to Admiral Wolseley :—

"ADMIRALTY, *May 12th,* 1827.

"DEAR SIR,—I am to acknowledge yours of
9th instant and cannot make any promises.
However I feel disposed to bring forward with
propriety as soon as possible your son, having
the most sincere regard for your excellent self.
God bless you, and ever believe me, yours most
truly,   WILLIAM."

The poor young officer whose claims the Duke
was disposed to bring forward, and who was
considered by Sir George Eyre, his late commander, to be so deserving of promotion, did
not, however, live to get it.   As previously
mentioned, he had to leave Rio Janeiro on account of the state of his health ; and after he
had been at home with his father for some
little time, he accepted an invitation from Sir
James and Lady Anderson, old friends of his
family, who had very kindly asked him to spend
some weeks with them at their place, Buttevant
Castle, in the County Cork.   At first, I believe,
his health was improved by the change of air,
but at the time he intended to have returned
home he suddenly became dangerously ill, and
was quite unable to take the journey ; and after

lingering for a few days he died, at the early age of thirty, on the 14th of June 1827.

Added to Admiral Wolseley's great sorrow at the death of his eldest son was also a feeling of deep anxiety about the future prospects of his other children. Neither of his daughters were at that time married, and his only surviving son was not then in any profession. In consequence of this, some months after the death of Mr. John Wolseley, he wrote the following letter to the Duke of Clarence :—

"Sir,—Since the period I had the honour of receiving your gracious answer to my application for the promotion of my son, Lieut. J. H. Wolseley, it has pleased God to remove him from this world. He fell a sacrifice to the climate of Rio Janeiro, where he served three years in the flag-ship, under my friend Sir George Eyre, and his untimely death has left me in a state of the greatest anxiety, as my two daughters may soon be left without competent protection. And my immediate object in now addressing your Royal Highness, is to state that my only remaining son (Cosby Wm. Wolseley) named after my uncle the late Admiral Cosby, has now completed his course of studies in Dublin College, is 21 years of age ; and was intended for the Church. But his dislike to that profession makes me anxious to provide for him in some other line of life. Your Royal Highness will excuse the partiality of a father, when I say that there is hardly to be seen a finer young man anywhere. Your Royal Highness was so kind when I had the honour of seeing you last at Bath, as to offer to get this son of mine a commission in the army, if I placed him at Sandhurst. But the strong repugnance of his departed mother to have both her sons in military professions prevented it. He is now unprovided for, and just entering life. I should end my days with satisfaction if I could see him in a situation to afford his sisters that protection they may soon stand in need of. And it is on his, and their behalf that I beg your Royal Highness will have the goodness, to provide for him in some way so that my wishes may be realized. And with his abilities, education, and attachment to your Royal Highness's interest, I have no doubt you would find him useful in your Household if there was a vacancy. I beg your Royal Highness will forgive my troubling you with this long letter, and hope for a favourable answer to my anxious request for this my only son. Relying on your Royal Highness's gracious friendship and goodness of heart, I have the honour to remain, your Royal Highness's much obliged and faithful humble servant,

"WILLIAM WOLSELEY."

The following is the Duke of Clarence's answer :—

"BUSHY HOUSE, *Decr.* 5*th*, 1827.

"DEAR SIR,—In answer to yours of 30th instant from Rostrevor I lament exceedingly the lamentable loss of your son. I can and do enter most fully into your natural and proper wishes respecting your surviving son, and wish he had entered the army, for then I might have served him. But however elevated my present situation is, I must not apply to Ministers, and really in my department there is not anything with his fortune he could accept.—Ever believe me, Dear Sir, yours sincerely,   WILLIAM."

Although this reply appears rather an unsatisfactory one, very shortly after the Admiral had received it, in the beginning of 1828, Mr. Cosby Wolseley was appointed ensign, or, as that rank would now be styled, sub-lieutenant, in the 32nd Regiment.[1] His commission was given to him by the Duke of Clarence, and was sent with an intimation that the gift was "a mark of his Royal Highness's regard and esteem for Mr. Wolseley's father." The Duke's kindness was deeply felt, and the regard of his Royal Highness was most warmly reciprocated by Admiral Wolseley.

[1] Mr. Wolseley some years afterwards exchanged into the 8th King's Regiment. He retired from the army in 1839 or in the beginning of 1840.

About two years later the Duke became King of England, King George IV. having died on the 26th of June 1830. The funeral, however, did not take place till the 15th of July; and Admiral Wolseley, by the new King's directions, was one of the naval officers invited to be present. He went over from Rostrevor to attend the ceremony, and was one of the admirals who were appointed to be "Supporters of the Canopy" that surmounted the King's coffin.

Evidently, before the Admiral received the invitation, private intimation was given that it would be sent to him; and I find among the papers concerning this event a printed notice, dated "Earl Marshal's Office, Whitehall Yard, 7th July 1830," in which it is stated that, by the King's commands, "the great Officers of State, His Majesty's Ministers, and the Officers of the Royal Household" were to appear in their "State Uniforms"; and that all officers of the army and navy attending the ceremony were to "appear in their respective full-dress uniforms, pantaloons and boots, with the mourning directed to be worn by them at Court, as notified in the *Gazette* of the 28th of June last." Next among the mementos of King George's funeral appears the following formal invitation, on paper with broad black edges :—

"EARL MARSHAL'S OFFICE, WHITEHALL YARD,
13*th July* 1830.

"The Earl Marshal has it in Command to request the attendance of Admiral Wolseley to assist at the Interment of His late Most Sacred Majesty of blessed Memory in the Royal Chapel of St. George at Windsor on Thursday Evening the 15th Instant at seven o'clock."

The Earl Marshal's regulations for the ceremony are somewhat in the style of a programme. They were printed on both sides of three half-sheets of paper, surrounded by broad black borders; and the three sheets are stitched together. From this document it appears that, unlike the state funerals of the present day, no princesses of the royal family appeared in the procession, or were apparently present in the chapel; and it seems rather strange that none of the bands of the regiments attended, and the *cortège* was preceded merely by their fifes and drums.

Obviously to prevent people who were uninvited from presenting themselves at Windsor Castle or at the chapel, "tickets of admission" were issued from the Earl Marshal's office; and Admiral Wolseley's ticket has been preserved among the other mementos of King George's funeral.

Seven o'clock was the hour mentioned in the

invitation; and probably those who were to assist at the ceremony were required to assemble at Windsor Castle at that time, although it is evident that the procession was not to leave until nine o'clock.

The Earl Marshal's directions for the funeral give a very fair idea of the style in which the ceremony was performed, and therefore I take some extracts from them. At the top of the first page, printed in large letters, is the word "Ceremonial," and immediately underneath is the following paragraph :—

"On Thursday Evening the 15th Instant, at nine o'clock, the Procession (having been previously formed in St. George's Hall) will move through the State Apartment, and the Royal Remains be conveyed to Saint George's Chapel in the following order :—

"Trumpets and Kettle-Drums, and Drums and Fifes of the Foot Guards.

"Drums and Fifes of the Royal Household.

"Trumpets and Kettle-Drums of the Royal Household.

"Knight Marshal's Men, two and two, with black staves."

Then were to follow the Knight Marshal's officers, the Knight Marshal himself, and the "Poor Knights of Windsor,[1] the officers of "His late Majesty's Household," the "Lords of the Admiralty, attended by their Secretaries"; and after them,

[1] Now called the "Military Knights of Windsor."

all the great dignitaries of the Church and the Bar, Privy Councillors, and eldest sons of peers, &c.

After them the "Banners of Brunswick, Hanover, Ireland, Scotland, St. George, and the Union Banner" were to be borne by peers; and immediately after was to come "The Royal Standard," followed by "Blanc Coursier King of Arms," bearing the Royal Crown of Hanover on a purple velvet cushion; and at each side of him, as his "Supporters," a gentleman usher. After them was to come "Clarencieux King of Arms," bearing the Imperial Crown of the United Kingdom, in the same manner; with his two supporters, followed by more dignitaries of the late King's household, who were immediately to precede "The Royal Body,—Covered with a Purple Velvet Pall, adorned with Ten Escocheons of the Imperial Arms, under a Canopy of Purple Velvet."

At the right side were to be, as "Supporters of the Pall, three Dukes, assisted by the eldest sons of Dukes"; and beyond them, at their right, were to be, as "Supporters of the Canopy, Five Peers, assisted by Eight Generals in the Army."

At the left side were to be, as "Supporters of the Pall, Three Dukes, assisted by two eldest sons of Dukes"; and beyond them, on their left, as "Supporters of the Canopy, Five Peers, assisted by Eight Admirals in the Royal Navy."

"Garter Principal King of Arms, bearing his Sceptre," with a gentleman usher at each side,

Q

was to follow. And the Marquis of Winchester bearing "the Cap of Maintenance," and the Duke of Wellington bearing "the Sword of State," were then immediately to precede

" The Chief Mourner, the King's Most Excellent Majesty, in a long Purple Cloak, with the Star of the Order of the Garter embroidered thereon, wearing the Collars of the Garter, the Bath, the Thistle, St. Patrick, and of the Royal Hanoverian Guelphic Order ; attended by His Royal Highness Prince George of Cumberland."

His " Train Bearers " were to be two Dukes ; and at each side, but apparently a little behind the King, was to be a Duke as " Supporter"; and following the train-bearers were to come " Sixteen Peers, Assistants to the Chief Mourner." Next to them were to come " The Princes of the Blood Royal "— " H.R.H. the Duke of Sussex," and with him " H.R.H. the Duke of Cumberland." Behind them " H.R.H. the Prince Leopold of Saxe-Coburg," with " H.R.H. the Duke of Gloucester." Each prince was to wear " a long black cloak with the Star of the Order of the Garter embroidered thereon," and was also to wear the Collars of all the different Orders possessed by him ; and " His Train " was to be " borne by two Gentlemen of His Royal Highness's Household."

After them the procession was to be ended by " a Royal Guard of Honour . . . from the King's Company, the Coldstream and 3rd Regiments of

Guards"; and following them "the Gentlemen Pensioners, with their axes reversed; and the Yeomen of the Guard, with their partizans reversed."

At the end of the programme it is stated that "the Procession was to be flanked by the Grenadiers of Foot Guards, every fourth Man bearing a Flambeau." Upon the arrival of the procession at St. George's Chapel, the trumpets and drums and the Knight Marshal's men and officers were to "file off without the door."

"At the entrance of the Chapel the Royal Body" was to be "received by the Dean and Prebendaries, attended by the Choirs of Windsor and the Chapel Royal," &c.; "and the "Procession" was to "move down the South Aisle and up the Nave, into the Choir, where the Royal Body" was to be "placed on a platform under a canopy of purple velvet, thereon escocheons of the Royal Arms, and surmounted by an Imperial Crown."

"His Majesty, the Chief Mourner," was to "sit on a Chair of State," at the head of the Royal Body; and their Royal Highnesses the Dukes of Cumberland, Sussex, Gloucester, Prince George of Cumberland, and Prince Leopold of Saxe-Coburg were to be seated near his Majesty the Chief Mourner."

"The Lord Chamberlain of His Majesty's Household" was to take his place at the feet, and the "Supporters of the Pall and of the Canopy" were to "arrange themselves on each side of the Royal Body.'

"The Peers bearing the Banners" were to be "arranged at each side near the Altar"; and "the Knights of the Garter present" were to occupy their respective Stalls, with the exception of the Supporters to the Chief Mourner," who were to be at each side of him.

"The part of the Service before the interment and the Anthem being performed, the Royal Body" was to be "deposited in the vault, and the Service being concluded, Sir George Nayler, Principal King of Arms" was to "pronounce near the grave the Styles of His late Most Sacred Majesty, of blessed memory."

These regulations for the ceremony were dated, "Earl Marshal's Office, Whitehall-Yard, 12th July, 1830." Probably a copy was sent to every one who was to assist at the interment of King George IV., and doubtless the whole of the "Ceremonial" arranged by "Norfolk Earl Marshal" was duly carried out upon the evening of the 15th.

Towards the end of 1834 Mr. and Mrs. Innes took a villa near Southampton for the winter months, and Admiral Wolseley and his youngest daughter paid them a long visit there, and before returning to Rostrevor, went to Portsmouth for a few days. A friend of the Admiral was captain of the guardship stationed there, and they spent an afternoon on board. It was the first time Miss Wolseley had ever been in a man-of-war, and after having spent so much of his life at sea, and having been in command of so many himself, it was, I believe, the last time the old Admiral was ever on board of one.

On the 10th of January 1837 he was appointed Admiral of the Red, in consequence, as it appears from a letter addressed to him by an official at the Admiralty, of " His Majesty having been pleased to order a Promotion of Flag Officers of His Fleet." It was, probably, the last promotion of flag officers that took place during the short reign of William IV., as the King's death occurred a few months later, on the 20th of the following June. Admiral Wolseley was at that time staying on a visit at Hilton Park, with his youngest daughter, Mrs. Madden, and her husband, Colonel Madden. In consequence of the King's invariable kindness to him, the Admiral was greatly attached to his Majesty ; and a lady who was also a guest in the house, and who was then a child of seven years of age, still remembers how much grieved and affected the Admiral appeared to be on the morning on which the newspaper arrived in which an account was given of the death of King William IV.

Of the remaining years of Admiral Wolseley's life there is not much to be written. He continued to live at The Anchorage, his little place at Rostrevor ; and after his eldest daughter, Mrs. Innes, became a widow, much of his time, especially during the summer months, was spent at Dromantine.

Towards the end of 1839 the Admiral went to Caen, with his daughter and her children ; and it was during the winter they spent there that the greater part of the little memoir from which I have so often quoted was written by Mrs. Innes from her father's dictation. It was, however, probably put away on the arrival of some friends who had been invited to spend some weeks with them, as it was apparently not finished till the summer, a part of which was spent by Admiral Wolseley and Mrs. Innes in Paris.

They left Caen about the end of April or beginning of May 1840. Admiral Wolseley was at that time entering upon his eighty-fifth year, and it was during this, his last visit to Paris that the fine portrait at Dromantine, which was considered an extremely good likeness of the Admiral, was painted by Jules Laur, a young artist who had shortly before exhibited a picture in the Salon, which, I believe, was thought by good judges to have been one of the best that appeared there that year.[1]

To allow this portrait, which was painted for his daughter, Mrs. Innes, to be finished, Admiral Wolseley was detained in Paris, I think, until the middle of July. He then returned to Ireland with his son, Mr. Cosby Wolseley, who had at that time retired from the army.

---

[1] M. Laur died, I believe, about three years after he took the likeness of the Admiral. If he had lived he would probably have been a celebrated painter.

The winter of 1841 and spring of 1842 were spent by Admiral Wolseley in London. His son, Mr. Cosby Wolseley, was with him, and Mrs. Innes afterwards joined her father and brother there. During the early part of the winter the Admiral was in good health, and used to drive in an open carriage in the park, with his daughter and her children, every day when the weather permitted. But about the middle of April the old wound, received so many years previously, when he so generously took the place of another officer at the storming of Fort Ostenberg, and which had since occasionally given trouble, again opened, and could not be got to heal.

The surgeons in attendance were of opinion that something still remained in the wound that should have been extracted, and it was consequently decided that an operation was to be performed. A jagged piece of lead about the size of a large pea, and some substance, thought by them to have been a piece of the cloth of the coat the Admiral was wearing at the time he received the wound, were taken from it.

Both the surgeons present afterwards expressed to Mr. Cosby Wolseley the greatest admiration of the great courage and endurance shown by the old Admiral during the operation, which must have been an extremely painful one, and in those days neither chloroform nor ether were ever used.

At first their patient appeared to be doing well;

but at his age such an operation, especially when
performed without any opiate, must have been
a very serious trial to the constitution, and after a
few weeks it became evident that the wound was
not likely to heal, and that he was fast losing
strength. The surgeons talked of performing
another operation, on the supposition that in the
former one they had not been successful in re-
moving all that was in the wound. But in consequence of the very weak state of the poor old
Admiral, they were afraid to undertake it. He
continued to lose strength from day to day, and
having about three months before that time completed his eighty - sixth year, he died, apparently
without pain, on the 7th of June 1842.

Admiral Wolseley was a man of strong religious
principles, and during the last years of his life,
when, from his great age, he was no longer able
to go to church, his daughter, Mrs. Innes,
generally read the Morning Service to him every
Sunday. And among the early recollections of
the writer, with every little detail distinctly im-
pressed upon her mind, is one of the venerable
old man as he sat slightly bending forward in his
arm-chair, one Sunday morning during their stay in
Paris, with his clasped hands resting on his knees,
while he reverently repeated in a low voice the
prayers and responses that her mother was engaged
in reading to him.

At the time of his death Admiral Wolseley was

at the head of the list of admirals of the Red Squadron, and was consequently the third senior officer in the navy, the Lord High Admiral of England and the Admiral of the Fleet being the only two officers above him.

It only remains to be said that the slight records still left of Admiral Wolseley's life show that he held a high place in the estimation of the distinguished commanders under whom he had the honour of serving, and that, evidently, that position was gained by his steady good conduct and strict performance of duty. He was also apparently, in consequence of the kindness and amiability of his disposition, equally successful in winning the affection and esteem of those who served in the different vessels under his command. And although his services to his country were not such as to entitle his name to a place on the long roll of British heroes who have gained immortal fame, and whose splendid deeds are historical, the records of Admiral Wolseley's life prove that he shared with conspicuous courage in the dangers of many a well-fought battle, and that he invariably distinguished himself whenever the opportunity offered.

Printed by BALLANTYNE, HANSON & CO.
Edinburgh and London

R

www.ingramcontent.com/pod-product-compliance
Lightning Source LLC
Chambersburg PA
CBHW020557030726
47497CB00007B/1977